MW01518724

The Day Immanuel Kant was Late

The Day Immanuel Kant was Late

Philosophical Fables, Pious Tales and other Stories

J. Mulrooney

188 Cassandra Books

© J. Mulrooney 2014

"Re-Statement of Romance" by Wallace Stevens from *The Palm at the End of the Mind* by Wallace Stevens, edited by Holly Stevens. Copyright © 1971 Holly Stevens.

Published by:

188 Cassandra Books
www.188cassandrabooks.com

188 Cassandra Books

Library of Congress Cataloguing in Publication Data
Mulrooney, J.
The Day Immanuel Kant was Late: Philosophical Fables, Pious Tales and other Stories / J. Mulrooney
2014950373

ISBN 978-0-9906991-0-1 (paperback)
ISBN 978-0-9906991-2-5 (ebook)

Contents

Acknowledgements

"The Day Immanuel Kant was Late" was originally published in *Fiddlehead*. "Philosophical Fables" was originally published in *Grammateion*. "Philosophical Fables: Leviticus 16:10" was originally published in *Dreams and Visions*. "When Judas Iscariot Left" was originally published in *Inklings*. "The Devil's Confession" was originally published in *Windhover*. "Michael's Pillow" was originally published in *New Oxford Review*. "Terry and the Moon and Me" was originally published in *Grail*.

"Re-Statement of Romance" by Wallace Stevens was published in *The Palm at the End of the Mind* by Wallace Stevens, edited by Holly Stevens.

I. PHILOSOPHICAL FABLES AND TWO OTHER STORIES

The Day Immanuel Kant Was Late

AS THEY DID EVERY YEAR, the weeds in the meadow announced the arrival of spring in Kœnigsberg. The earth rolled around to the right side of the solar system, allowing the sun its first direct look at the town in months. The weeds, sleepy and starved through the winter cold, exploded like Chinese firecrackers in the relative heat. They clawed and scrabbled upward as if to grab the sun and keep it all year long. At the same time, the cold entrails of the earth were loosened by the warmth, and the weeds stretched their roots down, sucking water and nutrients that the earth had locked away from them while it sunned its other hemisphere. The weeds do battle there in the ground. The stronger ones kill the weaker, and feed on their corpses, and grow stronger because of it.

On the first of the warm days that April, the little river ran gaily between its banks, laughing in its own secret language. Frau Hammerschmidt did the laundry there and hung it outside on a rope tied between two trees. The Pabel's new baby was crying with the lungs of an opera singer. The students at the university were writing their exams. Kapelmeister Haufbergen was practising a new fugue for Easter. The sparrows sang as if their hearts would break for joy, then disappeared to copulate in the evergreens. And Professor Kant was out for his walk.

He had changed from his woolens to his light tweed knickers, giving the new season a certain philosophical credibility. He carried a hawthorn stick with a brass handle. As he walked, he passed fixed checkpoints and the burghers set their clocks and watches. He passed at the same time every day regardless of the weather. He came to the meadow. The weeds were overflowing and fighting their secret fights. The ants were building a new city. Off to one side, near the path where the Professor walked, a single shy pansy began its life as a tiny green sprout, no taller than your thumb. The Professor came to the end of the meadow and passed the old elm tree. Up in their hive, a flight of honey bees prepared for their first harvesting run this year.

Fraulein Krause waited in the alcove for the scouts to return. In contrast to her companions, she remained still, fluttering her thin wings occasionally for warmth and shifting when one of the others crawled over her. She assumed the flight would be going out this morning. She could already tell it would be warm enough. But she gave no indication to the other gatherers around her. If the scouts came back and announced it was too cold, she would not even be surprised. It was a scout's job to tell the gatherers in the alcove whether or not they could work today. It was not a gatherer's job to think about it. The discipline of the hive came first. Fraulein Krause didn't worry about things until the hive made its demands. When the hive asked, she would do what she was told. Until it asked, she sat quietly and waited. Anything else was a waste of energy, and wasting energy did the hive no good.

The other bees were much younger than Fraulein Krause, and did not yet know how to wait. Some translated their nervousness into impatience, fluttering their wings and buzzing angrily, dancing about and complaining. Some felt the nervousness as fear, and they crawled up and down the walls of the alcove and each other and Fraulein Krause. The temperature in the alcove was rising now that the waiting bees filled it. They were all glad Fraulein Krause was there.

It was not just her size that they admired, though she was very large for a worker, and not just her experience, though of them all only she had been born before the last swarm. They admired most of all her quiet, which rose from her like perfume and filled the air around them.

The scouts returned and the flight left the hive. It was still early spring, and the coolness of the day cut the foraging short. Fraulein Krause made only two trips from the hive. The crop of flowers was not quite ready, and many of them had not opened enough to yield their food.

Despite the poor harvest, however, the day was judged a success. Spring had surely arrived, and with it the promise of abundance. Even nectar from the weeds was an event at this time of year. The young workers were eager to gather. The frightful shortages and cold of the long winter were over, and the grueling quotas of high summer not yet thought of. The light work of the day only excited the bees. That night they feasted on the last and best honey of the previous year. They danced until they could dance no more, for they were young and did not fear the future. Only Fraulein Krause would not dance. She sat off to one side and ate and drank quietly. If someone invited her to dance, she declined politely, using her large size as an excuse.

To the side of the dancing area the young bees boasted and argued, they drank too much and told jokes, they fell down laughing. They made fun of Fraulein Ungar, whose leg pouches were too small to carry a full load of pollen. Fraulein Ungar bragged that she could carry more nectar in her belly than the fattest of bees. They imitated beewolves, the terrible hornets that sometimes attacked the hive, by stretching their bodies and legs out and wiggling their abdomens when they walked. They told jokes about hornets' preposterous sexual habits, which were hopelessly disorganized and included laying eggs in the mud. When they had laughed and drunk their fill, they returned to the dances.

Alternating with the dances at intervals were speeches, since besides dancing bees prize oratory above all else. Some spoke of changing hive operations to improve efficiency, or giving greater benefits to those with harder jobs, some wanted job exchanges allowing gatherers to go back to work in the Queen's chambers and allow chambermaids to work the harvest, some proposed different methods of food distribution. There were political speeches about the wars with the beewolves or alliances with man. Some even touched on philosophical topics of broad interest, such as the possibility of knowing non-immanent truths. "All we know are our perceptions of the world," a handsome gatherer argued, "we cannot know what structure underlies the surfaces we perceive any more than we can know the thoughts of a bee who will neither speak nor dance. The real structure of the world," and she fluttered her wings for emphasis, "is hidden beneath the world we can see." When the speeches ended they all danced some more, or they argued about what had been said, and they flapped their wings and rubbed their front legs together, they crawled over each other and the dancers danced like fire.

Fraulein Krause was happy. She had felt very strong at the harvest today, but she was glad to relax and watch the dancers and listen to the speakers. She could hardly believe that she had once danced in the spring herself, that she had been a part of the spectacle before her this evening. The young bees shone with vigor and grace. It seemed to her that she had never seen such fine dancing in all her life, and that she could have watched it all night. She was disappointed when every dance ended and every speech began. But then during the speeches so many fine things were said, and said so beautifully, that she was carried away by them as well as by the dancing. By the time every speech ended, she wished the speaker would carry on forever, and she was sorry to turn her attention back to the dances when they started again. As the evening drew on, she could not decide which she loved more, watching the dances or listening to the speeches, and she changed her mind this way and that, depending on what was going on at the moment. And the beauty of both was heightened by her awareness of her own advanced age, the undercurrent that told her that this would be her last spring, and her gratitude for the life the hive had given her.

At the end of the night there was a play. The story was about a beautiful worker who uses her sting to save the hive from a band of beewolves, dying herself as a result. Before she dies, she tells the workers that she will live on in the flowers she has pollinated, in the trees she has fertilized, in the honey her harvesting has made. And she would live on in every one of them, she said, and every bee lived in every bee, for the honey that made them strong was collected by the other bees, so that they all lived on. A bee could never die, because all bees were one, all bees lived if only one lived, and that she was not really dying because the hive would live on, and she was a part of the hive. And when she died, a group of actors carried her off in a stately and mournful ballet, and Fraulein Krause wept for pity at the beauty of the play, and as she drifted down into sleep that night she thought that she would not mind dying so much when it was her turn, and she blessed the hive and everyone in it.

*

There is nothing soft or easy about anyone's life, thought Esther as she watched the first lightening of the eastern sky. It was high summer, and the weeds in the meadow where she stood were more aggressive with each passing day. They sucked water more quickly than she could, taking with it the nutrition she needed to keep alive. They spread their roots out wide and grew with incredible speed. Although they had not touched her yet, she could feel their tentacles grasping at her in the soil, ready to strangle the long delicate tubes upon which she depended for sustenance. They seemed a little taller in the beginning light, and a little more menacing. One day they would cut her off from the sun completely.

Esther herself was nearly five inches tall. She had five petals made of velvety deep purple leaves. Near the bottom of the lowest petal was a single large yellow spot. Where the petals met, at the centre, was her nectar tube, and her sex organs, the center of her being. Her purple corolla turned in the wind, and the warm breeze of summer took some dew from it as it passed. She stood a little taller and spread herself towards the spot from which the sun would rise.

Although the weeds were frightening, they were not worth worrying about, Esther decided. Nothing could be done about them. She could only grow herself, keep healthy and wait. She was waiting for pollen to come. When it came, life would be simple. She would make a seed. When the seed was made, she would be free. She could die in peace. But nothing had come in the night – the chances of a windborne arrival were remote. As she had done every morning since the springtime, she would make herself pretty again today and offer her body up in trade for the pollen she needed. She would be disappointed again, she expected, and retire, bruised, stained and violated, for another night of waiting. If only the pollen would come, if only the waiting would end, she thought.

Although she could control her physical fear of the weeds, the more subtle and delicate fears of waiting tortured her. Had she done anything wrong? Was there something more she could be doing? Were there no lovers left for her? At night, her fears became even more abstruse and superstitious. She worried that she did not pray enough, or that her prayers were spoken wrongly, or that some hidden fault prevented love from reaching her. But over the course of the summer, she had learned to rein in even these nighttime fears. She spent her spare time during the day composing arguments to be used to fortify herself in the night. Nature worked by certain unchangeable laws. Her life was subject to Nature. To commit suicide, to give up and surrender herself to her fears, would break the laws of Nature. Worse still, she thought, her action might set a precedent for Nature, and make suicide part of its law.

If her arguments were unconvincing, she was at least able to distract herself with the words until the dark of night gave way to the first blueness of dawn. Perhaps some message of love would come this morning.

Esther was both beautiful and fragrant, as her job required. She attracted insects from a distance. When they came near, she held out the promise of pollen and nectar. While they stopped to look, she searched them for pollen. Her clients – mostly bees and butterflies – started coming just after dawn and did not let her rest until dusk. They tore at her with their long hairy tongues until they had their fill of her nectar, or they scraped her until she was raw and sore and their pockets were full of her pollen. Now that the days were fine, so many came so quickly that there was never enough. She was always exhausted and trying to make more, and they would curse her and spit on her for not satisfying them.

Not all her clients were nasty. There were even some she liked. She liked the butterflies for their grace and beauty and lightness. But for the most part they were vain and not good company. The honey bees were not bad. There were strong quiet workers who were polite and had kind faces and honest eyes. She could even feel sorry for them as they probed and scraped her, sorry for their sad little lives, regulated in every detail, it seemed to her, by some tyrannic overlord hidden in an obscure fortress. Generally the bees took the food she supplied back to their hives, but some ate it themselves as they walked about upon her petals. Some became drunk and told her everything.

She did not like the talkers. They were full of self-pity and loved only to talk about themselves and their complaints, how the hive asked too much and they did not think they could continue, how their friends worked themselves to exhaustion and died, how they themselves would soon collapse under the grueling work schedules. To Esther, they were incomprehensible. If she had wings like they did and she didn't like something, she would simply fly away to some place where no one could ever touch her.

But she was rooted to the spot, and there was no sense worrying about wings. She searched all the insects, the ones she liked and the ones she didn't, hoping that through them some one of her own kind had sent her some message of love, and she could create a seed. The first bee of the day had arrived.

*

As he walked, Professor Kant crunched the windblown leaves of autumn underfoot. Soon it would be time to change back to his woolens. He stepped off the road and onto the path that led through the meadow. The weeds and harsh grasses there had already strangled the few flowers that had grown in the summer. They were ready for the long sleep of winter, their time of dormancy and hiding.

The Professor saw a flash of purple among the weeds and squatted down to pluck it. As he raised it to his face, a large honey bee rose from it angrily and jabbed its sharp poisoned sting into his cheek. The professor let out a yowl and brushed at his face with both hands. He caught the thorax and head of the bee, separating them from its abdomen and sending them flying into space. The stingered belly hung, still wriggling, in his cheek. He grabbed it between his forefinger and thumb. It was damp and soft, difficult to grip. He squeezed too hard as he pulled out, crushing it into a wet pulp between his fingers. He flung it away without looking at it. His left hand already had a handkerchief ready, and he wiped his fingers and applied the handkerchief to the wound. Then he continued his walk. He pulled his watch from its fob and looked at it. He began to walk a little faster.

In the meadow, the flower he had plucked lay with the crushed abdomen of the honey bee. The bee's head and thorax lay some distance off. A small troop of ants found the parts and took them home to feed their families. Soon the earth, leaning like a tiring top, had spun Kœnigsberg a little further from the sun, and the winds picked up and the snow began to fall. The weeds felt the cold, but they were clever enough to trap the dead leaves and flowers as the wind blew them. They made them into a blanket, and the snow only added to its warmth. The weeds sent their roots down deep into the dark earth so that the cold could not reach them while they slept. They snored in the darkness of the cold ground, and if they ever woke, they cursed the fickle sun and the cold season, they mocked the flowers and leaves that had been more beautiful than they were in the summer but were now dead and warming them with their corpses. Underground, the ants slept and worked sporadically, they kept air and water and food in the soil. They fed the weeds and tended their roots, for the roots kept the soil strong for their houses. By the time the earth had rolled back to face the sun, the dead honey bee had been completely consumed by the ants, and the dead pansy was nothing more than a mulch for the weeds to eat. Eat it they did, and the sun smiled down and the earth rolled around, and that is probably why the weeds are still standing in that very meadow today.

Philosophical Fables

Upon those that step into the same rivers different and different waters flow.

Heraclitus, Fragment 12

HERACLITUS IS STANDING in the river. He steps up on the bank. The river flows on, and swirling in it are the gold, yellow, red and orange leaves of autumn. He steps back into the river and thinks: It is not the same water. He spots a poplar branch on the little waterfall to the north and watches the water kick it out of place and bring it to him. It brushes off his shin with a little tickle and floats south, migrating, perhaps in pursuit of the leaves it held in springtime. Winter will be here soon. He slaps at the water as if to catch it or stop it flowing. Everything changes. Everything always changes.

As Heraclitus walks up the hill, he is thinking: No one can stop the river or hold it still. Last month I fished in this very spot, and it was easy to think that the fine trees and warm sun of summer would last forever. Now summer has passed. The water in the river is not the same as it once was. The leaves rush to the sea, as many as the dead. They come, they go, they are replaced. Even I am replaced. In not ten years, every cell of my body will have changed. I am not the same as I was. I am a river without banks, a hole through which the time of my life runs like the water.

He braces his back against a tall jack pine and rubs. The scratching feels good. He pads along the leafy ground and yawns. He walks home slowly, tired.

*

The cold winter comes and even the river freezes. The spines of straight-up trees have crystallized somewhere in the ice, twisted and turned like Salvador Dali's watches. A frozen snow has hidden the dead leaves of autumn, obliterated them. They never existed. The riverbank where Heraclitus stood and wondered is as still as a painting. Nothing is moving anywhere. Nothing ever moves. But deep in his den, Heraclitus is wrapped in a bed of dead leaves and cool dark earth, dreaming of the springtime and fishing in a river that flows on forever.

Simon And The Economy Of Salvation: A Moral Tale

IT HAD BEEN CLEAR TO SIMON since he was very young that he was special. His mother, standing above him in her brown corduroy skirt, had said, "You're a special child." He had overheard her tell others the same thing. "My boy Simon. He's special. He's going to accomplish something."

From the earliest, Simon acted in ways that befitted his specialness. He ate only certain foods and violently objected to others. He was attracted to various ascetic practices like cold showers, early mornings, and fasting. He read science fiction novels and watched public television. He remembered all his dreams on awakening, and they all prophesied greatness. In school he loved science and mathematics especially, ever since he had received a gold star for being the only student to discover that both 11 and 7 were possible last numbers to the sequence 1, 2, 3, 6. His progress through life, as he saw it, would be described by the ascent of the x=y curve:

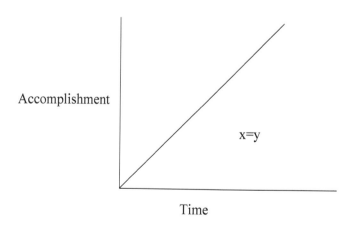

He would be a rocket blasting off from the *tabula rasa* of infancy into the cosmos of the intellectual and political elite.

As his studies progressed through high school and his marks blazed to the top of his class, he began to realize that he learned things better and quicker than anyone he knew. His own talent shocked him. If he just put his mind to a problem, in a very short time he would solve it. The universe was a great explosion of intelligibility. The forecasted ascent of the x=y curve seemed at the very least a conservative estimate. Every day brought him some new accomplishment. He seemed to be increasing geometrically, a comet destined for the farthest reaches of space. Nothing less than the x=y² curve could describe him:

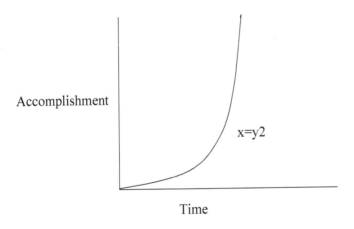

His destiny was infinity, and he would soon be heading very nearly straight up.

Simon sat in the last row of benches at his graduation. In fact, he was the last person in the last row. The high school diplomas would be handed out in order of academic merit and his provincial gold medal was the grand finale. His former girlfriend, Gloria, sat in the second to last row directly in front of him.

"I thought you loved me," she whispered, leaning back over her bench.

She was a tall thin girl whose chest had developed late, but with a vengeance. She was not very bright, Simon thought. Certainly she was not as bright as she had seemed before he had slept with her. Simon whispered that Gloria should never think he didn't love her. "But I've changed. You've changed. We've grown apart. We need to be free to grow, to accomplish new things. I'm going away to school and I can't be worried about a hometown sweetheart. You're going away too."

Principal Flaff stood up at the podium. "You can be justly proud of what you have accomplished, young people,..." he said.

"But I'm willing to wait for you. And we can see each other most weekends, we won't be that far apart," said Gloria.

Gloria's eyeliner was running down a cheek in a blurry stripe. It was hot in the assembly hall, and sweat combined with the emotion of graduation had ruined the makeup of many girls. "We'll have to study. If you want to go to law school, you have to work. I'll be doing physics. You can't just take weekends off and accomplish anything at university. It's not high school."

"Even though you sometimes had to work harder than you might have liked,..." said the principal.

"I thought you wanted to marry me."

Simon had said so, it was true. But he did not mean it anymore. It was obvious that things said at certain moments in life were not binding. He did not explain this to Gloria, however, whom he knew would be incapable of

understanding.   Instead, he told her he did not know
whether he still believed in marriage as an institution. "Did
you know that just last week the *Globe & Mail* reported that
sixty per cent of all marriages end in divorce? And marriage
is the sure death of love, I mean, love-making, I mean that,
sexually..."

"I would like to turn the microphone over to a special
young man,..." said the principal.

"Simon!" cried Gloria, and sank off her bench to the
floor sobbing noisily. The graduates and parents in Simon's
area craned their necks to see what was going on.

Simon leaned forward over Gloria's bench. "No, no,
honey,..." he hissed.

"Simon Cyrenian!" announced the principal.

Simon rose and walked down the centre aisle to the
podium. Gloria's grandmother, who was ninety years old
and almost deaf, said, "Oh, isn't he handsome?" in a shrill
voice. Gloria's noisy sobs and the titter of a girl in grade
eleven reached Simon at the podium. "He was always a
special child," his mother announced in a loud stage whisper.
He took a deep breath and gazed across the hall. He left the
copy of his speech in the pocket underneath his gown. "We,
the new graduates, the class of nineteen-_____, would like to
take this time..."

Simon worked like a demon at university and became a
great scientist. He published a breakthrough monograph in
quark theory as a graduate student. It won him a large
research grant from the government. He almost took it. But
he knew the history of physicists in our time. He knew that
they, like the great lyric poets of old, make their only
contributions while young and then die. Or they spend the
rest of their lives polishing their single narrow insight. He

had no intention of dying young, nor did he plan to spend the rest of his life adding decimal places to the conclusion of his article. His graph was still on the rise, but gravity was tugging at it. The research grant would turn his flesh to stone. He was not going to become an old physics professor living off a discovery he had made at the age of twenty-two. He told the committee he was not interested.

"That's right, Simon," said his mother. "You don't need them. You do what you think."

Simon received his doctorate two years ahead of schedule and left the university. He had in mind a new kind of accomplishment. Albert Schweitzer had combined a career as a doctor, musician and critic with some humanitarian interests. Simon made up his mind to follow in Schweitzer's footsteps. He would become a warm humanitarian as well as a great scientist. A few inquiries put him in touch with the World Peace Through Jesus organization. They were thrilled to have a young man as accomplished as Simon with them, and agreed to take him to Africa and pay all expenses.

Although the World Peace Through Jesus organization usually required its members to attend months of prayer group before sending them on trips, they made an exception for Simon who was eager to begin and was able to convince them that he was an exceptional case. Some meetings, however, were unavoidable.

"God's plan for us is an economical one," said the preacher. He had already been talking for thirty minutes.

Come on, Jack, I have work to do, thought Simon. In fact, he did not actually have work to do, he had a dinner date with his girlfriend Melissa. He thought that the preacher might have shown a little more consideration, though. He might just as well have had work to do.

"Every being in creation has its purpose, yes, every hair on your head has been counted by God, and, rest assured, every hair has been put there for a reason." Here the preacher, who was bald, patted the top of his own head. The congregation chuckled politely. "Yes, from the most accomplished," here he looked gratefully at Simon, who was looking at his watch, "to the least accomplished," and he looked at Spanky Colloton, the crippled half-wit who was the organization's poster child, "yes, we every one of us play some part in God's grand economy of salvation." He paused to wipe his head.

The service droned on for another hour. Simon whispered his apologies to Mrs Hall, his spiritual adviser: "It's just that I have to get back to the lab tonight,..."

Mrs Hall said he was a busy young man.

"It's not that I wouldn't love to stay, you understand."

"That's all right, Simon. You go and do your work. We understand."

Simon snuck out the back as the congregation began to sing: "Someday, he'll make it plain to me. Someday, when I his face shall see..."

He got to the restaurant nearly forty minutes late for Melissa. She had been crying, he could see. "I can't believe you're leaving," she said. "After all our plans." She was wearing a low-cut blouse, and the waiters leaned over her as they walked past in a way that Simon found annoying. Melissa, he decided, had no class.

"Plans have changed," he said. "I'm not going to be trapped in a university wiping undergraduate noses for forty years. I've got things to accomplish."

"And what happens after all your accomplishments? Are you assumed bodily into heaven? Do you win a prize? Does Jesus Christ pin a medal on your chest?"

Simon could not remember what he had ever seen in Melissa.

For a full year, Simon travelled through impoverished areas of Africa, teaching local bureaucrats, missionaries, and businesses how to use computers. Some had purchased the computers themselves. Some had received them as gifts from the generous folk of wealthy nations. Simon found some of the poor Africans were easier to teach than others. One tiny village he visited had no electricity and the computer components remained in their shipping boxes in a hut. Simon took them out of the boxes and showed the people that the power cords made useful rope and the installation CDs diverting toys. One of the women used the boxes to hold potatoes and dishes.

More often, the Africans did have electricity and he spent his time showing them what the computers could do, or he fixed breakdowns with tiny screwdrivers and clever fingers. The work would have been dull, but Simon found the location and people exotic and interesting. He learned Swahili words for several types of plant and once shot at a lion from the back of a Land Rover. He ate strange foods from wooden bowls. He squatted on his haunches. He learned to pass the hot afternoons in the company of mysterious old blacks who spoke in ways unclear to him and laughed when nothing seemed funny. He had his mother send him some anthropology books, and after that learned to fit in quite well. Sometimes he even ventured a joke, and once or twice a man laughed.

Simon was pleased with the whole trip. He felt he had become a humanitarian as well as a scientist, making a not insignificant contribution to the sum total of good will and understanding throughout the world. "The trip to Africa is a success," he wrote his mother. "I feel I am growing as a person here." Everything was going just as he had planned. But something was missing.

Then the best thing that could possibly happen happened. In Gabon, Simon contracted malaria and almost died. The trip acquired an element of drama and existential earnestness that had been lacking. Simon had just arrived at Lamberene that evening. He was sitting on the ground teaching the names of the stars to some old black men, who smiled and laughed and nodded. Then he was lying in a bed between white sheets, shivering and wetting himself. He fell asleep and was haunted by dreams of cannibals, vampires and corpses. When he awoke, a nurse appeared and cleaned and fed him. He slept again. When he next awoke, a slim black doctor in a white lab coat stood beside his bed.

"Well, well, you're awake," said the doctor. He had an American accent. "And very lucky, too. How do you feel?"

He felt bad.

"You're lucky to be still with us. Not many go down so low and come back up. You know you've lost something like forty pounds in a little more than a week?" he asked absent-mindedly. "I guess you still have things to accomplish in this world." He spoke a little about different regional types of malaria and the different vaccines that were effective against one strain but not another. "Where were you before you came here?" he asked.

Simon told him.

"Yes, well, there you go. I'll be looking in on you a little later." He wandered out of the room.

Simon lay in bed for nine weeks. The hospital was a small brick building in the middle of a small town. For a time his primary recreation was looking out the window, which he did eagerly. He was amazed at the sheer substantive presence of the people who walked by: small black boys in cut off trousers and bare feet, slim women in faded cotton dresses with bones more loosely articulated than white women, neat young men with heads almost shaved to baldness who came and went at all hours. They all had such interesting eyes, he thought, sometimes hooded and expressionless, then bright and squinting with laughter, then sharp and observant. He looked at them as if he had never seen people before.

It was pleasant to be under the dispensation of illness with no pressure to accomplish anything. He found an old Calculus textbook and solved the problems to pass the time. He felt that the malaria in his blood was a sign that Africa had truly touched his inner self. He read some books on near death experiences, and toyed with the idea of developing a new value system. "I have learned how precious life is," he wrote his mother. "Every new day is beautiful. Perhaps that lesson is the greatest accomplishment of all."

He also toyed with the nurses. His favourite was Roberta, a tall dark black woman with breasts that rivalled any Simon had seen in the Western hemisphere. When he was strong enough to be moved, Simon said good-bye to her.

"I don't understand," she said. "When you got better, we were going to Canada together."

Simon was grateful to Roberta for giving him something to live for when he was sick, but he had recognized that his feelings for her could be no more than gratitude. They were from different worlds, and not meant to be together. She would forget him quickly once he was gone, he thought sadly. "I'll send for you once I settle some things there," he said.

Simon returned to Canada.   He was warned against recurrences of the disease and told to live a slow-paced regular life. He began to carry a hawthorn stick, and when someone told him Glenn Gould used to wear fingerless gloves, he adopted a pair. He saw *Casablanca* on late night television and bought a new trenchcoat.   He went to university fêtes and his mother's society parties and adopted the attitude of a man who has seen it all. He decided he could bring a new perspective to science and wrote to Waterloo asking about research grants and a professorship.

In the meantime, he wrote a book about his experiences in Africa called *In the Steps of Schweitzer.* He wrote of the beauty of the African people, the unending fascination and validity of their cultures, and how we could all learn something from them. The climax of the book was all about his infection and how he would have died had not the Africans gotten him western medical care. On the advice of his publishers, he included a chapter about the sexual practices of certain tribes, drawing material indiscriminately from anthropology texts, his experiences with Roberta, and *Penthouse Forum.* Although his advance was not as large as it should have been, the book sold well and he made a small reading tour across Ontario. That would have been the end of it, but the next year the World Peace Through Jesus sued him for philandering when he should have been bringing world peace through Jesus. He brought a counter suit against them for censorship and violation of civil liberties and settled out of court. The book was re-edited and reprinted with a new title, *Sex in the Steps of Schweitzer.* It hit the *New York Times* bestseller list and Simon made Oprah Winfrey and Donahue in the same month, where he appeared on a panel that included professors from Stanford.

Simon's mother did not live to see her son on the Donahue show. She had had a stroke the month before and lay in the hospital, critically ill.

"I'm going to be on Donahue, Mother," Simon said.

"You're a special boy," she said, but her left side was paralyzed and it came out "Yurplby." Simon smiled and nodded and called the nurse for a bedpan.

He sat by her bed every day for a week listening to her mumble and pouring her apple juice. One day she shouted loudly and convulsed, then died as Simon watched from a vinyl chair across from her bed. That night Simon cried until he slept. As he watched the sexton fill in her grave, he told himself that it was over and he would have to get on with things.

Simon's publishers sent him to the Andes to live with the tribesmen there. The trip was a failure, however: Simon could hardly speak their dialect and the tribesmen were surly and rough. One night they found him in bed with one of their young girls and threw him off the mountain.

When he returned home, Simon suffered a malarial relapse and was bedridden for two months. At night, his nightmares and delirium returned. He was standing on the porch of his mother's house when a hospital bed bumped down the staircase. Two clawlike hands with long black nails reached from under the covers and pulled the sheet down, revealing a white face.

"Hello," said the face. Its eyes popped open. They were bulgy and staring and cracked like broken glass.

"Hello," said Simon.

The face turned into his mother's. In the confusion of the dream, she also became one of his Calculus professors. Her claws gripped a Cartesian graph with an elaborate curve on it. "What equation is this?" she said.

Simon had been doing calculus problems to relax during the day and recognized the graph. He named the equation.

"What equation is this?" asked his mother, holding up a similar graph.

Again, Simon told her. "Two DX by DY cube-root I twenty-three."

"Very, very good," she said in a cloying way that made Simon feel he was seven years old again. "And what graph is this?" She held up the $x=y^2$ curve.

Simon was embarrassed to be caught out in his own vanity. He became shy and giggled nervously. "Well, Mother,..." he began, looking down. His mother rose from her stretcher. She wore a brown corduroy skirt.

"This," she said, in the same tone she used to scold him, "is the $x=y^2$ curve. It describes," she slapped the page, which was now on a flipchart, "your life." A great clod of earth rolled from her mouth and fell into her blouse. She paced back and forth. "Now this equation advances upward and outward infinitely, but its upward advance is geometrically greater than its outward advance. In fact, as you grow older, Time will seem to increase at a snail's pace while Accomplishments multiply. How old are you now, please?" Her nose crumbled off her face into a muddy ball. She continued pacing.

"Twenty-eight, Mother," said Simon.

"Twenty-eight. Right. So within a few years Accomplishment will be advancing almost infinitely upward." Her legs collapsed under her into a heap of dirt. She balanced on the stumps and fixed a cracked gaze on Simon. "You think you're special? You think you can stop the advance of time?" Her leprous body began to disintegrate into earth. "You think your fate is infinity? You will never reach the temporal axis of your own decline? The temporal axis of your own death? You?" She began to gibber and shriek, and as she did she collapsed entirely into a mound of earth, no bigger than a grave. Her voice echoed up the street as Simon stood alone looking at the little mound. "You?" He swept up the dirt so the neighbours wouldn't see.

Simon became an associate professor in physics at Waterloo and taught a journalism course in travel writing. He became paunchy and thin-haired and married a timid and flat-chested graduate student from Idaho who could cook and make a martini that tasted the same every time. He expanded his student monograph into a book, bolstering his youthful ideas with better documentation, graphs, footnotes and measurements.

"The ideas might be good," he told his classes, "but real scholarship requires thorough documentation. As Thomas Edison said," and he looked down from the podium to indicate that, but for an accident of time, he would have beaten Edison to it, "yes, as Edison said, genius is ninety-nine percent perspiration and only one percent inspiration."

Simon was convinced that he had something more to say about quarks, but found himself unable to get much beyond what was already said in his book. He had worked hard at research when he arrived, even sleeping in the lab as he had done in his old student days. But he became weak easily and the doctors told him he ought not to work so hard, the only thing he would accomplish was another relapse. Over the years, his once mighty self-discipline crumbled away like his mother's corpse in his nightmares. The research went nowhere. Early mornings became excuses to fall back asleep under warm sheets. Cold showers became hot baths that lasted an hour at a time. The graph trending infinitely upward became a crooked path leading nowhere. Simon's birthdays came and went and time advanced at an aimless, mundane speed. The letter announcing his promotion to tenured full professorship stayed on the kitchen counter for a week before he bothered to open it. He felt like he was sleepwalking through his life but was unable to awake.

One winter night when Simon was lecturing in Toronto, he met his old girlfriend Gloria in a bar. Even in her heavy coat, Simon could see she had retained her figure. At first she did not remember him.

"Simon Cyrenian. High school. You know. Your old boyfriend."

She began to remember.

Simon asked her if she had read *Sex and Schweitzer*, he would be very interested in her opinion, and was she in Toronto long, he was just over teaching at U of T, of course there was his research and a new book, but maybe they could get together, talk about old times, you know,... Simon ran his fingers up her knee and along her thigh. He noticed a mark below one knuckle where his wedding band usually was and changed hands. "What do you say, Gloria," he whispered in her ear. Her blonde hair was moussed and touselled and smelled of perfume. He needed her, he decided. "I was at my best with you," he whispered. "Everything's been a mistake. We should have stayed together like you wanted. Sure, I've got everything, I've travelled, I've written books, I love my research, but accomplishments just don't matter to me without you. What do you say. Gloria." Simon saw a new world rising before him. They would move to Switzerland, Gloria would fix him drinks, he would go to CERN and write a new theory of elementary particles.

Gloria smiled. "What did you say your name was, honey?"

Later that night, Simon was thrown out of O'Toole's for trying to hit one of the student drinkers. The air was cold and full of snow. He waited for a cab for ten minutes before deciding to walk. His anger warmed him, but the alcohol made him sleepy. The snow covered the city like a white sheet, and three blocks from his hotel Simon fell into a snowbank to fall asleep forever.

EPILOGUE IN HEAVEN

When he awoke in the dreams we dream in our final sleep, he took his complaints to the Lamb. "Why did you ruin my life?" he cried. He remembered for the first time in a long time his vision of himself at his best. He remembered a relentless mathematician, a knight of self-discipline, an indefatigable seeker of knowledge. As he showed the Lamb the $x=y^2$ graph, he choked with love and sympathy for the man he had almost been. "Why was this taken from me? What did you leave me?"

The Lamb sighed. He looked in his briefcase and shuffled about. He looked at his watch and pretended to be fascinated by a bird that flew past. He asked about Simon's mother, and commented that the day was very fine.

Simon would not be dissuaded. He ignored the Lamb's dissembling and asked his question again. The Lamb sighed again. It was clear Simon was not going to become frustrated and leave. Finally the Lamb pulled a dusty piece of paper from his briefcase and began to unfold it. It was a graph. The x-axis was labelled Time, and the y-axis was labelled Accomplishment. A name was written in neat capital Letraset letters at the top: "SIMON". The graph showed a haphazard series of points, so chaotic they might have been random. The Lamb set it up on a flipchart.

Simon looked along the Time axis to see how the graph corresponded to his memories. There was no consistent agreement. Accomplishments he was proud of might be rated indifferently, poorly, or well with no clear pattern. Happy times were indistinguishable from sad times, brilliance indistinguishable from mediocrity. Although he had lived the data on the graph, he recognized none of it. "Surely there's been a mistake?" he asked.

The Lamb shook his head sadly.

Simon was almost in despair. He took out his calculator and tried a few things, but none of them was any good. Only an equation of infinite complexity could have generated the crazy series of points. Just looking at it made him nauseous. He gave up trying to analyze the whole graph and focused instead on the y-values where Accomplishment was highest. There was a gold star at the highest point around the age of thirty-four.

"What is that?" he asked. He could remember nothing about that period of his life that would warrant a gold star.

"That is how you got here," said the Lamb proudly as if here was something he knew a lot about. He nodded approvingly at Simon, then at the star, then at Simon again.

"Yes, but what is it?" Simon asked.

The Lamb deflated. He became evasive again. "You won't like it," he said.

"What is it?" Simon demanded.

"You won't like it," said the Lamb.

Simon was becoming angry. "What is it?"

The Lamb avoided Simon's eyes and concentrated on pulling the graph off the chart while he spoke. "One day," he said, "you walked past a little girl's window on the way to work. She liked your hat very much."

"My hat?" said Simon. The Lamb nodded. Simon tried in vain to remember the hat. He couldn't believe it. "My hat?" he said again.

Simon's mother appeared. "You can't talk to my boy like that. He's special. He's accomplished something."

But the Lamb had wandered next door and was talking to the neighbours. "My hat. My hat was the gold star." Simon sat for a long time trying to remember either the little girl or the hat, but he never could. For a long time he was pissed off. But after a while, he got used to it. He moved into his mother's mansion, and from what I hear, they lived happily ever after.

The goat whose lot was marked 'For Azazel' shall be set before the Lord, still alive, to perform the Rite of Atonement over it, sending it out into the desert to Azazel.

Leviticus 16:10

OHOLIAB, THE SMALL HILL GOAT from Israel, sits upright with legs crossed in the smoking car sipping tea from a delicate china cup. Unlike the goats we usually meet in these parts, his hair is newly coiffed and oiled, and a small yarmulke is held neatly between his ears by two bobby pins. The faint smell of Brut aftershave mingles with the goaty smells. He is wearing a paisley ascot with an old purple morning coat.

"In those days," he began, "when I was younger than I am now, we were kept in a big pen of about forty, prisoners, as has been the lot of our race since Adam and Eve fell from Paradise." He had lived in the old country, or at least Brooklyn, and he said his THs like Ds - in dose days. He had a singsong way of talking.

"Right after I was weaned, my mother – may she rest in the palm of God's hand – was taken from us, hung from her ankles, and slaughtered. Of course, I was just a young kid and I didn't for a long time figure this out, because although many were led out never to return again, we never spoke of what happened to them. In fact, with a prophetic instinct that is now marvelous to me, I remember I thought then standing at the cedar gate that I some day would follow her.

"Still, that didn't come until later. I was speaking of my days in the pen. Well, God gave us to the Israelites to be their flock. He could have given us the constipation too, so I don't complain.

"Our goatherd was named Ehud. He was a long-limbed man with curly black hair. We hated his dogs – they gave us fleas and urinated everywhere – but Ehud we loved. He knew where the best pastures were, and the freshest springs. He would find them always for us. Even when we complained and wanted to stay in some sunny field, Ehud would laugh, frighten us a little with his staff, and herd us all off to better grazing. We were the fattest and sleekest goats in all Israel.

"Well, we were not unhappy in our prison. Young people today think we were cowards because we were not revolutionaries, because we were not political, because we did not stand up for our rights." He spoke these words broadly, with contempt. "So revolution and politics and rights make the world so good. Oy! That's why everyone is so happy, because of politics.

"But we were not free, they say. Freedom Americans love so much they put it on their licence plates. But we were free. We had plenty eats and drink, and shelter, we mated in the spring – what else is freedom? Perhaps you will say we were sentenced to death. We would die arbitrarily, with no say in it. But when the Angel of Death comes and knocks on your door, see if you are free to say no.

"Well, unlike political men, we never forget we are going to die. It was our destiny to be captives, it was their destiny to be captors. We grew strong and fat eating the meal they prepared for us, drinking from their troughs, grazing the pastures to which their goatherds led us. You're going to die sometime, right? So if it's a little sooner, a little later, you want to live to be ten thousand? Who needs to be constipated for such a long time?

"So anyways, one day the high priest's men come to get me and I think, say good-bye, Oholiab, the Angel of Death has come to visit you. As was our custom then, the others of the tribe don't say a word to me and I don't say nothing to them. I'm a young man and I'm going to go according to the proscribed forms, even if I don't know why. When you're young, you can make yourself do things.

"So the men come in and I stop myself from screaming and running when they put the rope around my neck to lead me out. The funny thing is, since I'm not screaming, I'm pretty soon not scared at all, I'm just wondering what it's going to be like and what they do. Would they sing, and would I hear it, I'm wondering, if you can believe that. We all loved it when they sang. And so that's what I'm wondering about as I'm led to the slaughterhouse. But you know kids! They're young and stupid, and what are you going to tell them anyway?" He waved a front leg to indicate that there was nothing you were going to tell them anyway. He took a sip of tea.

"So, thanks God, they didn't take me nowhere near the slaughterhouse. What I'm wondering is, why not, but you can't argue with some people. They take me to the river, which is flowing very dirty and deep because the rains have just ended, and they dunk me in and say prayers over me. The water is very cool at that time of year, and it's night, so I'm very cold. In fact, I have a bit of lower back pain even to this day, and I blame it on that cold river on that very night.

"They take me to watch their religious service, which is very elaborate and beautiful, with all sorts of costume and finery. I've just been chilled but up at the front with all the priests and the great crowd watching, it's very hot there, believe me when I tell you. The ceremony drags on and on, and they sprinkle all the people with the blood of one of my tribe, Yshroel, who had this funny way of scratching but was otherwise a very nice-looking young fellow, not like some of those I see around nowadays. I almost get sick when I realize it's him, but for some reason I think I'm a British soldier and I have to stand at attention and so I just stand there. I start thinking again about what it will be like when I hang from my ankles and they let the blood drop out of me, whether it will be fast or slow, whether it feels like giving blood to the Blue Cross or not. Of course, I'm half delirious by this point, what with the chill and the heat and excitement and what-have-you and so on. I was in none too good shape, I'll tell you that."

Here he stood up slowly and refilled his teacup. We younger ones tried to get a look at his throat to see if it had ever been slit, but of course he always wears that paisley scarf as an ascot in his morning coat, so we couldn't see. With a number of sighs and oohs and ahs, he plopped down in his seat, spilling half his tea in the process. He swung his slippered feet under the table and belched loudly, like an Arab.

"Excuse me. I'm not so young as I once was before I got so old.

"Anyways, the priest puts his hands on my head. At first I flinch because his smell is strange and oily, but he begins to chant and I stand still to listen. Hypnotized. I don't remember what all he chanted because he's speaking the ancient tongue, and besides he's not talking to me he's talking to God, and who am I to eavesdrop on such things?

"Then he lays his hands on my head and chants more, but to me and to the people. His hands seem to weigh a very great deal, and I'm wondering what he's doing. It feels like he's pushing me through the floor, but I don't see any pushing. His hands are just resting on my head. Later I learned that he was putting all the sins of his tribes onto me through his hands. Perhaps I was just tired you'll say, or delirious, or he really was pressing on my head. But I was there. I felt the weight. Those were sins, and was I as old then as I am now, I would not have been able to stand under them, they were so heavy.

"How heavy is a sin? I don't know. I carried so many so long I don't remember anymore how much each one weighed. Some more, some less, like rocks.

"A lot I don't remember so good. The lights all disappear and I'm walking with a fine rope around my neck, it's dark and I'm falling asleep, but I stumble behind a strange man who takes me far out into the desert. All I want to do is sleep, but no, the shmegge drags me up by the rope and pulls me on. It's very cold, I'm telling you, at night in the desert, and I try to walk close to him but he runs away and whips at me with the rope. I'm falling asleep anyways, miserable and cold, and I stumble on beside him.

"Next thing I know it's bright daylight, I'm in the shade of a big rock, and I'm all alone in the middle of nowhere at all. He abandoned me in the middle of the desert. Now I remember I have a mission: find Azazel. That's what I remember from the chanting the next day: find Azazel. Actually, even in those days my memory was none to good.

"I walked around that desert for a long time. I walked everywhere, carrying those sins across my back like a packhorse. I would walk up to everyone I saw to see if they knew Azazel, and no one touched me because the priest had laid his hands upon me. It was like I had the mark of Cain on my forehead. Who ever heard of everyone for so long leaving a small hill goat such as you see before you alone, I'm asking?" He rolled his head and eyes to show us no one had ever heard of it. "But of course, I never found Azazel neither.

"I walked for a thousand years. I walked from Lake Semechonitis to Luxor, from the mountains of Moab south to Tyre, I walked through the cities of men and herds of goats and sheep, and I feared no lion nor wolf. On hot days the sins weighed me down until my coat burned like fire and I panted like a dog, but I always walked on. I circled the Dead Sea and wandered the length of the Nile, I saw all the banks and beaches of the Red Sea, but I didn't find nothing.

"Actually, I thought of maybe publishing a travel book of my journeys some time. Maybe I could make a little money that way. Like Thor Erikson, or whoever that travel writer who makes the popsicle-stick boats is.

"You know, I almost despaired many times on that journey – Who wouldn't have? – but the sins, like a fat gadfly, kept me walking. Even when I had the gout I kept walking. But what can you do? You got a mission from the priest. You got to walk. And so I walked.

"So then one day on my way across the desert to Jordan, I meet a young rabbi. He looks none too good, this fellow, like he hasn't eaten nothing in a while. So I offer him matzos, which I always carried some in my pockets, but no, he's fasting, he don't want none. 'Suit yourself, you want to be so skinny,' I say and I eat. He's watching me kind funny, and I think, 'Uh oh, smarty, better keep a close eye on Mr Hungry.'

"I'm watching this guy close, and I roll my matzos up into my pocket. He's still staring, like I'm Marilyn Monroe or something. So I say, mostly to keep his mind off things, 'Hey rebbe, you know which way is Azazel?' And his eyes nearly pop out of his head. First I think he's going to eat me, priest or no priest. Then it turns out he was waiting for me. Of all the people everywhere, of all the goats and wolves and sheep and lions and camels, only this guy knows what the hell I'm talking about.

"We talk for a little while. He says that now he's going to find Azazel and I don't got nothing to do with it anymore. Which is fine by me, only I got approximately twelve tribesfulls of sins on my back, can he do something about that?

"So he takes the sins off my back. I can walk like a normal goat again instead of all stooped, except I've got a bit of a swayback from it all, but still, I'm so happy I can't believe it. I want to sing and dance. I thank him a thousand times before he tells me to get lost because he's got to go look for Azazel, and that he'll send for me when everything is all finished up. Then I go on a bender so I can't see straight for a week afterwards."

Oholiab had become very animated as he got to the end of his story, and was perspiring noticeably in his excitement. We were worried he was going to have a stroke right there. But the excitement seemed suddenly to drain out of him like blood. He slumped forward on the table and sent one of us for more tea.

"Then what happened?" we asked when he had refreshed himself.

He looked old and confused. "Oh, a lot of things," he said. When he gave no sign of continuing, we asked him some more questions, and got similarly dull replies. He brightened a little when we asked where he was going.

"To visit the rabbi," he said. "I got a postcard from him."

"Peoria!" the conductor sang. His voice was harsh and nasal. "All for Peoria out here!" Oholiab dropped his teacup. "Oy! My stop!" It shattered on the linoleum floor and he kicked the remnants under the seat beside him. Grabbing his briefcase, he hopped to the door with more agility than you would have thought he had in him.

"Good-bye, my friends! Shalom!" he called, then mumbled "Or does one not say that here?"

We watched him stroll down the platform, a short skinny little goat from the Middle East in a purple morning coat with tea stains on his paisley ascot. The elbows of his jacket were shiny with age. Soon the rush of the crowd swallowed him up, and the train began to roll. The whistle blew twice and the diesels roared, and the rest of us were quiet all the way to Chicago.

The Heart of Ernest Bodkin

ERNEST BODKIN, WHO WORKS in one of the tall buildings downtown, sits on the toilet feeling sick. From his heart to his bowels there is an unbearable pressure so that he feels as if he must burst. He ate too much pineapple and banana tenderloin, cooked for him by his fiancée, Julia. Julia is no longer really his fiancée, however. Ernest has been trying to tell her this for the past six months, but she refuses to take the point.

Besides the food, Ernest also swallowed too much wine. He leans forward, elbows propped on knees, staring at the rough plaster wall across from him. The dinner candles seem to dance in front of his eyes although there are no candles in the bathroom. He rocks from side to side on the toilet seat to see if pressure might ease. Perhaps Julia has poisoned him. Were he not feeling so sick, the thought might excite him.

Outside the door Julia is waiting for him wearing lace leggings and a black camisole that accentuates her bust. This thought also fails to excite Ernest, a clear sign that he is sick.

Something inside him falls. The pressure in his chest suddenly moves downward. His rectum is pushed open to a huge size, it spreads and burns. He pushes. Sweat forms on his forehead and drops down his nose. Just when he feels the pushing must make the veins in his temple burst and the stretching split him in two, the pressure stops and the stool begins to slide easily. His rectum closes with a noisy fart, and a large splash soaks his buttocks. He immediately feels better. He slumps forward on the seat and relaxes, brushing the sweat from his face and panting. He wipes himself and stands up, adjusting his pants. He looks behind him, as he has ever since he was a child, to see what he has done, as if his mother were still looking over his shoulder and about to say, "Oh Ernest, what a good job." Ernest's friends sometimes say of him that he never came to terms with his mother, whatever that means.

Music begins to play outside the bathroom door, something with a tenor saxophone. Ernest does not listen. He is looking down into the toilet bowl. He sees a bright shiny red ball, about the size of his fist, covered with blood and bobbing jauntily in the yellowed water. It throbs in time with Ernest's pulse. It is his heart.

Ernest went to Julia's apartment that night to make the final break with her. He had decided to be firm, harsh if necessary. "Julia," he planned to say, "we both know this isn't working. It cannot continue." He decided on the formal 'cannot' instead of the usual 'can't' so that she would know he was serious. He drove angrily through the downtown traffic on his way there practising his short speech. "It cannot continue," he said, racing a red light. An opposing truck making a left turn jerked to a stop and honked.

Six months ago he had told Julia that it was over, that he did not want to see her anymore. He had driven her to her parents' house for the weekend and was about to make the trip back to the city. He stopped the car by the creek, their usual trysting place, but left the engine running. He turned to Julia and said, "I think we shouldn't see each other anymore."

To Ernest's credit, the comment was not altogether unprepared. They had not been getting along well for several months before that. He had stopped taking her out to meet his friends, telling her "Boys' night out" or, more often, nothing at all. There was a great fight when she found out that there had been more boys' nights out than she had been aware, and that Ernest's friends' girlfriends and wives often were along. Ernest and Julia had fought several times since then, each threatening to leave the other, he threatening more often than she. Generally she backed down and gave in. She would become quiet, let the fight fade away, and say, "I guess I love you more than you love me." Which, he had to admit to himself, was true.

But he was not ready for the ferocity of her reaction that night in the car by the creek when he said, "I think we shouldn't see each other anymore." She began to cry. She put her head down on the dashboard and wailed. She pulled her hair. She hit her forehead against the dashboard and the uprolled side window. She screamed. She sobbed, "Not tonight, not tonight, oh Ernest don't leave me tonight."

It was horrible.

Ernest turned the engine off and began soothing her. He gathered her to him and held her close, repeating quietly, "I won't leave tonight, not tonight. Maybe not ever," and stroked her hair and face. Her skin was hot and wet. Eventually he comforted her, and they sat in the front seat, she leaning on him, folded in his arms. She seemed precious to Ernest in the car that night, a delicate flower threatened by too strong a wind. They sat in the front seat in silence, looking at the trees and brush swaying lightly above the water. Julia sniffed from time to time and rubbed her face. Ernest dropped his hand slightly so that it rested on her plump breast. He began to fondle it. She looked up at him. There were tears in her eyes, and a fearful questioning look. It made her look precious indeed, but Ernest began to feel uncomfortable, so he leaned down and kissed her. She closed her eyes and kissed back. As he pulled her shirt open, it occurred to Ernest that this might not be the best idea.

He did not call Julia that week. He went to work early and stayed late. He cooked elaborate meals for himself and spent the rest of the evening cleaning up his small apartment and doing the dishes. He listened to sad songs with titles like "Keep on Loving You" and "Nothing Compares To You" and remembered all the girlfriends he had had up to Julia. Soon he had placed Julia among the ranks of the old girlfriends and he thought of her with a warm regret and nostalgia, as if she were someone he had loved long ago who had died and gone to a better place. On Friday night he borrowed several pornographic DVDs from a man at work and drank too much while he watched them.

One night the next week Julia was in the lobby of his office building after work. At first he was suspicious. He expected that she wanted to fight, or that she was going to do something ridiculous like give back the presents he had given her. To his surprise, she seemed happy. He also noticed that her hair had been done, that she wore more makeup than usual, and that instead of her usual baggy jeans, she wore a short tight-fitting skirt. He noticed the changes with approval. He saw in her a new confidence, a self-sufficiency. He saw in her a new sexiness.

"We're going out to dinner," she said gaily, taking his arm. "I'm buying."

Ernest studied her for signs of shrewishness or nagging, but there were none. She was not asking him out to scold him or complain. She no longer needed him, he thought with pleasure.

Julia hummed to herself and laughed. She led him to her favorite restaurant, where they talked about work and friends from school who were getting married. They drank a bottle of wine and began to giggle about times they had wanted to have sex and almost been caught. Ernest could not remember the last time he had had such fun with Julia. He began to regret breaking things off with her, although he knew it was the right thing to do.

Women, he thought, amazed him. Ernest often thought of himself in the third person, which felt more solid and objective than the first. Julia had grown more and more possessive over their months of troubles, and more and more irritable. And now here she was, reconciled to their breakup, laughing and drinking as charmingly as when he had first met her. Perhaps all she had needed was a good cry and a final round of sex (Ernest thought of sex like boxing, and in his mind referred to "rounds" and "bouts" of sex). They had not had sex for at least a month when they had had their good-bye round in the car by the creek. Sex relaxed him, he thought.

It was not until they were ordering dessert that Ernest discovered things were not as he thought. Julia's cheeks were flushed with wine and happiness. She said, "Oh Ernest, I'm so glad that we're not breaking up anymore."

Ernest's heart dropped into his stomach and acid splashed in his throat. He did not understand. He said nothing.

"I promise to be better. I know I shouldn't be so worried about the time we spend apart." She took his hand and rubbed her new red nails along it while she talked.

Ernest wasn't listening. He was horrified. While Julia talked ("How good she was going to be! How much better their new life together! How much love could grow!"), Ernest tried to find his mistake. He had thought that everything was over after their night by the creek. He tried to think how she could have gotten the impression that he did not want to break up. He could not remember anything. Then he realized: Julia had taken literally all the words he had told her while she was crying. She took their final love-making as a reconciliation. His heart dropped down into his bowel.

Julia was so happy at the restaurant that Ernest had no heart to tell her things between them were over, although he was sure that they were. He did not want her to begin that horrible screaming in the restaurant. In bed with her that night, Ernest resolved that he would put an end to their relationship.

Over the next six months Ernest let Julia know that his position had not changed: they were still breaking up. She became suspicious and resentful again, and Ernest neglected to tell her where and with whom he had been. He met Julia for dinner two or three times a month, but often came late and sometimes did not show up at all. He resented her intractability and her possessiveness, and longed to be free of her forever. He could not think of what he had ever seen in her.

There was a great improvement in one aspect of their relationship: in bed. Julia's resentment and determination to hold him made her passionate and aggressive. Beneath her clothes Ernest discovered a surprising variety of undergarments that never failed to drive a new stake of lust through his heart. Although he had initiated sex most of the time in the early phases of their relationship, Julia began to take over. He might return from the bathroom to find her half undressed, strutting like a girl in a beer commercial. She grabbed him in restaurants and whispered hot wet kisses into his ear. In bed, she began to take an interest in his penis, an organ she had formerly eschewed with ladylike reserve. She growled at him, and they scratched and bit and fought.

And besides sex, they did have good times. Ernest was, he knew, a charming fellow. He remembered birthdays and opened doors. He easily picked up checks and handled acquaintances at restaurants and bars. He always had a new theory on self-improvement, which he would declaim with boyish enthusiasm so that even people not much interested – such as Julia – were beguiled. He worked steadily at his job, and always had money in his pocket. He recognized his steadiness as one of his most attractive qualities.

Mostly, however, they bickered. And that was why, a few hours before he would sit hiding in Julia's bathroom, Ernest Bodkin was driving through the downtown traffic practising his speech. He would step inside, say, "Julia, we both know this isn't working. It cannot continue," stand in stolid silence while she screamed at him or cried, and then leave. He understood that he did owe it to her at least to let her scream at him. He had resolved to let her scream and cry. This time he would speak no words of comfort, he would not take her in his arms. He would stand and bear up his part until she was through, then say good-bye and leave. He realized that he should have ended things six months ago in the car by the creek, that it was his fault that things had been dragging on, that as things stood this relationship was no good for him nor Julia.

While he said that it was his fault to himself, however, he did note that it was important to see both sides of the issue, and had to admit that it was partly Julia's fault too.

Julia could not understand Ernest. It had been nearly two years since they had begun seeing one another. At first she was the reluctant one. She had gone out with a boy in university who had cheated on her every summer, as she discovered when he passed her a sexually transmitted disease one passionate September evening. She had not wanted to get involved with anyone, at least not seriously. Then she met Ernest.

At the time they worked in the same office building, and at first met only for lunch. He was always cheerful and talkative, and he made her laugh. Their lunches, infrequent at first, became more common. Several times they ran into each other by coincidence, and Julia began to suspect that he watched for her. He later admitted that this was true. Her old boyfriend had made excuses not to see her. Ernest's clumsy scheming was touching and flattering.

His conversation was entertaining as well. He was always on about some pet topic, and he would keep talking for hours at a time. Although she rarely listened carefully – there were always too many details, and his ideas were impractical – she found something in his enthusiasm touching. It was nice to find a man interested in something other than himself. Little by little she gave herself to him, his charm slowly finding its way through her reserve. From the first time they slept together, he began to propose marriage constantly, in a tender, joking way. Julia, who had begun to think that she had found a man she could spend her life with, was thrilled. Instinctively, she did not let Ernest know how much he moved her. She told him he was silly, which he was. He was exuberant and passionate, and she began to love him for it. She began to feel that her destiny was complete, and that they would live together forever.

Almost as soon as she admitted to him that she would like something permanent, however, his passion cooled. He became withdrawn and quiet. Instead of lying in wait for her, he now stopped returning phone calls, then made excuses. In the days when he arrived early to all their meetings, he had told her that coming late was an attempt to show power. Now he was always late. When she asked him about it, he told her not to be so stupid.

Julia could make no sense of Ernest. She had not changed in the least. He had changed. She began to think that there must be another woman, but Ernest told her that she was silly to be jealous. But if there was not another woman, why had Ernest changed? She went to a fortune-teller in the attic of a downtown house and was told she was unlucky in love and would die young – this fortune only confirming what she always suspected. On the radio at work she heard a folksinger sing,

> The sailors are dreaming of riches
> While the merchants dream of the sea.
> Tonight I will go to bed dreaming
> Of one who does not dream of me,

and she had to go to the bathroom and cry for half an hour on the toilet seat. She decided that she would not let the other woman have him without a fight.

When Ernest arrived at Julia's apartment ten minutes late, she was not ready. She answered the door breathlessly wearing only high-heeled slippers and a towel. She had just taken a shower, would he wait while she did her hair? Dinner would be ready soon, she had a tenderloin in the oven. He thought he was going to say he would not be staying for dinner, but he found himself saying that everything was just fine. One of Ernest's problems, he recognized, was a strong desire to please people. He sat on the couch and drank while Julia did her hair and dressed. He felt no desire to take Julia to bed just then, and was pleased with himself for this. He was strong. He would not need to be as harsh as he had planned. He and Julia could talk like adults and continue to be friends. Perhaps they could even sleep together once in a while. He recalled a line from a song that had been popular a few years before: "But we still sleep together once in a while." Their relationship was simply moving to a different level, a freer, more mature level. Whatever she was cooking smelled good.

Julia appeared at dinner wearing a camisole that accentuated her bust and made Ernest's groin hop. He had to admit that despite all their fighting, their relationship seemed better now than it ever had before. While they ate, Julia licked her lips and her food suggestively, wiggled in her chair and leaned forward so that Ernest kept catching glimpses of her breasts.

Normally Ernest would have responded with growing excitement, but tonight his stomach was off. He continued to eat, but his heart was not in it. He barely noticed Julia's provocations. By the time Julia brought out the dessert, Ernest was feeling definitely sick. A great pressure had built in his chest that traveled down to his stomach and bowels and back to his chest again. He excused himself to go to the bathroom.

And so Ernest stands looking down at his heart floating in the toilet bowl. The heart is not the shape of the hearts in Valentine's Day cards and advertising billboards. It is round and bloody and valves stick out of it like obscene tumors. Ernest wonders if he should pick it up, but a long aversion to sticking his hand into toilet water prevents him. He feels his chest, taps it lightly, punches it. It sounds hollow. He leans down to pick up his heart, but a sudden knock comes on the door and Julia's voice calls, "Ernest, are you all right?" and he jumps to attention, not wanting to be caught in a disgusting act.

"Just a minute," he calls.

Around his lightly beating heart float the small pieces of shit that he excreted with it. The water is very yellow – that would be the wine. He wonders for a moment if the heart isn't supposed to be the sort of organ that you really can't live without, like the brain only not as smart. Ernest did not take biology past grade ten and can't remember. Perhaps the heart is more like an appendix or a fingernail, something that people lose all the time. He feels well enough, in spite of his agitation and the smell. He decides he will go to the doctor for a physical soon, and with that puts the medical aspects of the case from his mind. He reaches into the bowl and grabs the heart. It is slimy and cold and repulsive to touch. With the suddenness of a living creature, it squirts from Ernest's squeezing hand and plunges back into the toilet. Cold urinous water splashes up into his face.

He turns to the sink and washes his face. First he has to wash his hands – he can't wash piss off his face if he's got piss on his hands, he thinks – and turns back to the toilet. But now the heart is underneath a small ovoid piece of shit. The smell of his own indigestibles is beginning to nauseate him, and he stands up to open the window and turn on the fan. He wonders: how best to move the shit and grab the heart? It occurs to him briefly that this is a strange situation, him reaching into the toilet to get his heart out so that he can go back and join Julia in the living room.

It is the sort of thing that always happens to him, he has noticed. Last week he brought eggs home from the grocer and one of them was broken. He takes a fresh package of toilet paper and opens it, placing all four rolls on the sink. The week before that, he bought a shirt at Eaton's that was missing a button and had to be taken back. He puts his hand in the cellophane wrapper and fishes in the toilet. Random variable misfortunes, he calls them, silly little problems that happen to one out of a hundred people always seem to happen to him. He is the one out of a hundred. He knocks the shit off the heart and is holding his excreted organ in his hand when Julia bangs on the door again. Ernest jumps and drops the heart. Again it splashes into the toilet bowl.

"Ernest, what's going on in there?" Julia calls. "Are you sick?" Ernest told Julia he felt a little sick before he went into the bathroom.

"I'm fine," he says, leaning over the toilet bowl, reaching for the heart again. He sounds fine. It is true, he feels fine, too.

"Well, what are you doing in there?"

Ernest can't think of anything to say except Just a minute, which is what he says: "Just a minute." Julia startled him, and he notices that in the toilet the heart is beating faster. Now it is swimming in a little circle around the bowl like a toy boat, bumping the pieces of shit out of its way as it pulses around.

He succeeds in pulling the heart from the toilet and places it, still beating, in the sink. He is wondering what to do with it now. He can't very well put it back the way it came out. It is too big for him to swallow. He opens his shirt to look for some opening nearer to where he wants it to go, but there is only his navel, which is closed. Outside the door he hears Julia pacing. The saxophone music has stopped. "Ernest, what's going on in there?" she says. She wants to know if she should call an ambulance.

Ernest puts the toilet seat down and sits on it. He stares at his heart in the sink. There is no way he could hide it in his pockets, especially beating as it is. He thinks of asking Julia for a plastic bag, but he doesn't want it to suffocate, and besides, she would want to know what it was. He sits for another few minutes, rubbing the back of his neck and staring at the heart in the sink. He feels quite well. Perhaps it is a mistake. Perhaps it isn't his heart at all. Maybe it is just a big red piece of shit. But it is beating in time with his pulse, so Ernest is forced to conclude that this is unlikely.

Outside the door, Julia calls again. He makes a decision. He stands up, lifts the toilet seat, and, coolly picking the heart out of the sink, drops it into the bowl and flushes it away.

Julia is in tears when he emerges from the bathroom. "What were you doing in there? I thought you had killed yourself! I was about to phone the police." He has been in the bathroom for more an hour, he discovers.

He tries to calm Julia down. She is so agitated, he decides that he ought not to broach the subject of their breakup immediately. He begins to tell her about creative schizophrenia, his new theory of self-improvement.

"Creative schizophrenia means suppressing part of your personality in the right circumstances. When you're at work, for instance, you can't think about sex or you'll never get anything done. Arthur Schroedinger, who was a famous physicist, had sex all the time – except when he was doing physics. You see, you have to get part of your personality right out of the way, and then you can use other parts. Probably the best time to do physics is right after you've had too much sex, so that you don't think about it. It's a split personality thing. Creative schizophrenia."

Julia, who is still agitated, does not listen very well. "Oh Ernest, you don't even know what schizophrenia means. It's a disease, not a split personality. And why isn't every rapist a great physicist, then?"

On many occasions, Ernest tried to explain his theories of self-improvement to Julia. Her inability to understand was, in fact, one of the reasons he decided she was not the girl for him. Ernest always thinks of the girl he is currently sleeping with as "the girl for him." Julia held that title longer than anyone else.

Because Julia is cranky, conversation quickly stops. It is still early and Ernest has nothing to do at home. Julia is too unfocused to break up the relationship now. Ernest decides to seduce her.

He felt rotten about it all the way home. He realized the way Julia's mind worked: she thought that sex meant their relationship was continuing. She was unable to see sex for what it was: sex. It was not a promise of future dinners and conversations. Women were sentimental that way. Ernest had been offered a transfer to Vancouver, and decided to take it.

*

Julia would spend nearly a year in black despair after Ernest left her. She lost weight. She went to bars and met men with whom she once would not even have spoken, men in their thirties or forties who listened to loud rock music while driving their cars too fast, men who later in life would purchase clothbound books of the poetry of rock musicians and smoke marijuana with their children's friends and their embarrassed children. She slept with these men.

One day while she was cleaning under the loveseat, she found a photograph of herself and a man. She did not recognize the man immediately. When she did recognize him, she could not remember his name. When she remembered his name (it was Ernest), she realized that he held no power over her anymore. He had ceased to exist for her. She looked out the window, and a brilliant sun was shining over a clear spring morning. Many things would happen to her in the years following, things she had prepared for and things she was unprepared for, but nothing that was too much for her.

Things went well enough for Ernest after "the Julia affair", as he thought of it. I wish I could say the business with the heart made the slightest bit of difference, but it really didn't. He married a girl from Washington state and they had a nice boy who once was tried for assault but they hung the jury and nothing came of it. Ernest got elected to government as a Liberal, or perhaps as a Conservative. He lived the rest of his life surrounded by admirers and friends, and died peacefully in his sleep at the age of 102.

Ernest's heart floated through Lake Ontario east down the St Lawrence and out into the ocean. Still beating, it managed to avoid all the nets of the fishermen. When it was just a little beyond the eastern edge of the Grand Banks, it began to sink. It was a particularly tough little heart, and it sank like a stone. On the bottom of the ocean it lived, eating snails and shrimp and the clear eyeless fish that roam the eternal darkness of the sea. It was last sighted by a Masonic bathosphere two hundred miles west of the North Mid-Atlantic Ridge. Apparently it has gotten stuck under a rocky embankment where it continues to beat despite Ernest's death. It lives by luring small innocent creatures to itself, where it sinks its jagged teeth into their flesh and eats them. It has been there for a number of years, and it seems likely now that it will be there still when Christ comes again.

II.   PIOUS TALES

When Judas Iscariot Left

FOREWORD

There are two things I should like to say before we begin. First, while it is possible that universal salvation is God's plan, I certainly would not want anyone to think this means that he is dispensed from any Christian obligation. Second, while the end of time may prove the devil to have been a coward and a dupe, he is not to be underestimated. Today the Prince of the World remains very much with us.

THE STORY

SATAN must have fallen asleep, because he did not hear anything until the shoes were right beside the rock. He was startled and struck with a sudden fear, as if the Enemy had caught him off-guard. Then he thought more rationally: This is still Hell, and I am still master here. He thought about leaping up from his rock and growing again into a huge and bloody-winged tyrant to terrify the poor blockhead standing beside him. He almost moved, but the work of imagining himself in a new shape was too much effort, and he decided against it.

It occurred to him that he did not know who this new person was. He had believed he was alone in Hell. Perhaps it was the Great Betrayer come back. He thought of calling – sometimes he called him "Jew-Ass" – but was more comfortable not calling. The shoes had off-white rubber soles with blue canvas uppers. He could not remember what kind of shoes Iscariot wore.

The shoes walked out of Satan's line of vision, and he listened to them thup-thupping around his rock. The fact that he was beneath the rock and the person in the shoes did not know it suddenly struck him as funny, and he had to suppress a giggle. Soon the shoes came back to where they started and turned away from him. It was possible to make out the brand name on the heel: "Keds".

"Hey!" Satan yelled, as the rock above him pushed down into his head and chest. The person above the shoes had sat down on it. Satan pushed up on the rock so that it shifted.

"Oh my," said the voice from the shoes. The weight went off the rock and the shoes turned to face Satan. The rubber was peeling around the sole on the left shoe.

"Mm," grunted Satan, settling down into the stones beneath his rock again.

"Is that you, Dark One?"

Satan was delighted that the voice knew who he was. He put on his deepest, most impressive voice and said "Who is it who asks?" He had not spoken in a very long time, however, so his voice cracked like an adolescent boy's on the second 'who'.

If the Keds noticed, he could not tell. "A servant," they said.

"A servant," Satan said. This was a good answer. Over the ages, he had had to endure rebellions and challenges to his leadership from every quarter. Near the end, he had taken to napping beneath the rock just to avoid all the annoyance. It was nice to meet someone who knew his place. It was necessary to reinforce that knowledge. "A slave, you mean," he bellowed, and this time his voice was prepared and he could feel the ground quiver with fear beneath him. "Bring me," and he described a particular goblet made from the skull of a city planner who had been stabbed to death in a housing project. "And fill it with blood and flesh so that I may eat and drink my fill."

The Keds disappeared over the ridge in the direction of the treasure rooms.

Satan wondered vaguely where the new slave had come from. When Judas Iscariot left, he thought he was alone in Hell. He had watched Judas go, disappearing through the rusted gates and into the mist over the river. To his surprise, Satan had experienced this final betrayal with a kind of relief. With no followers, he could relax a little. He was no longer on display, no longer had to enforce discipline, no longer were there a million millions waiting his every word. Alone, he had shrunk himself down to a small size and pulled the rock over on top of him. And there he lay, flat on his back, for ages and ages.

He had been beneath his rock so long that his body had made a comfortable indentation in the stones he lay upon. He stared at the surface of the rock above him, worn smooth by his head rubbing against it. Turning his head beneath his rock had been all his movement for many ages. If he turned to his left, he could see one of the old blast furnaces, now cold and dark, and the gate through which Judas had left him. If he turned to the right, he could see a small stretch of wasteland rising to a hill and, far in the distance, the tips of the turrets of his own black fortress. He liked to look at the furnace and the turrets and dream of his power. Sometimes he thought he would like to go again, to cross Hell and see his treasures and palaces, to fly to Earth, now restored to its prelapsarian state, and rain fire and terror upon its pointless inhabitants. He always decided not to. It was nice beneath the rock. He was pleased that the Keds now made any trip unnecessary. He must remember to ask the name of his new slave – not out of respect or interest, but because names gave you power and someone to accuse.

He was dozing and had forgotten all about the slave when he was awakened by the sound of feet scraping against the ground beside him. Looking out, he saw the Keds.

"I have brought your cup," they said.

This was a triumph for Satan, who had not had a trustworthy servant for a long time. He almost pushed the rock off and stood up, but decided not to. Why show himself to a slave? But there was the problem of getting the cup under the rock. "Pour the cup out onto the ground," he commanded.

Knees and calves appeared as the Keds squatted. A long slim hand reached down. There was the goblet that had so delighted him when he first received it. There were rubies in the eyes and a diamond in the nose, and the top of the skull had been sawn off and glued back in upside down to make a cup. Yet somehow it was not as beautiful as he had remembered.

The liquid from the cup trickled over the rocks around Satan, and whatever came near him he sucked up and swallowed with the smaller rocks around him. He had not had anything to drink in a long while, and he could not place the flavour.

"There was nothing to bleed," said the Keds, "so I gave you red wine."

"Mm," hummed Satan. Wine was not as tasty as blood, but it was something. He decided to overlook the incompetence. "Bring me," he commanded, and asked for a poisonous black flower that grew in the thorns near the gates of Hell.

The Keds brought the flower and some thorns, and Satan ate them from the ground with some of the stones and gravel in which he lay. He began to wonder again where this new slave had come from, since he thought everyone had left him and there was no new world from which to acquire new objects – or had a new Creation begun and he been given again authority over its inhabitants? He had not been keeping up with the news, and he had no spies. There were many questions he wanted to ask, but he was afraid that he would lose face if he did not know what was going on. Finally he said, "Why are you here when all the others left?"

"Because,..." said the Keds.

But Satan was embarrassed that he had asked a question. "Not out of allegiance," he interrupted. "Of all the pitiful creatures in the land, you alone were too frightened even to leave. You are worthless and weak," the devil said, "and barely fit to be my slave.

"Your file was burned," he continued, "and your name blotted out from all eternity. But if you tell me who you are and where you are from, I may create a new record of you. Do not think," he warned, "to lie to me, for I know the hearts of beasts, men, and angels, and my anger is terrible."

The Keds shuffled and above them there was a sniff and cough. "My name is Michael," said the Keds. The voice was small and sad. "I don't have any other name here. I have not been on earth for a long time."

Satan cringed at the name: St Michael the Archangel had thrown him from Heaven before Time began. But he did not show his discomfort to his new slave, who of course could not see him underneath his rock. "I will call you Stink," said Satan magnificently, like a king conferring a knighthood. "And you shall be my slave." And he gave Stink a new task to carry out, more jewels to bring him from one of his palaces far on the other side of Hell.

*

The ages passed and Stink and Satan lived together in
Hell. During the days (or what passed for day in Hell) Stink
worked on renovations that Satan ordered while Satan dozed
or chewed the rocks on which he lay. Satan's view was soon
obscured by the hobby horses, tools, and equipment that
Stink left around his rock, but the degraded view was more
than compensated by his anticipation of a new Hell. Satan
discussed the changes eagerly with his slave, now insisting on
a style of arch, now deferring to Stink's judgment regarding
species of thornbush, now confirming some detail of
landscaping ("the morass will be on the *west* side of the new
swamps..."). During these conversations he forgot himself
completely and spoke to Stink as if he were an equal or a
friend, and he always reminded himself to be particularly
severe later.

Satan was particularly impressed with Stink's blasphemies:
Stink kept suggesting improvements that mimicked Heaven.
This palace would be like the Archangel Gabriel's, this
temple to Satan like Michelangelo's new one for St Peter,
this jungle like the forests tended by St Francis. "Brilliant!
Brilliant!" Satan would cry, and rub his hands together
beneath the rock in anticipation and glee. What could be
better than to show the Enemy that you could do him one
better? When Stink suggested a biographical series of
paintings of Satan based on those cloying Stations of the
Cross, Satan was so excited he told him that he "wished
Stink were a devil too," so that he would be "fit to rule" with
him, the Great Satan. He meant it too, at the time, although
it was a little silly, when he thought about it later.

Satan insisted that Stink feed him three times a day, but
when Stink came Satan asked so many questions that he did
not have time to eat and his food dissipated into the gravel.
He would ask again and again how the addition to the palace

was coming, was the courtyard marble as black as before, what were the temperatures in the blast furnaces and kilns, how thick were the new walls? Although his only comments were grunts and threats ("I hope so, for your sake"), Satan was delighted with Stink's progress. He had begun to feel again a little of the excitement of ownership, and looked forward to the day when the work was done and he could assume his rightful throne in a magnificent new palace. Stink had worn the bottoms completely off his shoes, and sometimes after work he put his feet in the gravel by the rock to let Satan lick the blood.

When evening came, Stink and Satan played checkers. Stink would report the further progress of the work while the devil, peering out at the board on the ground from beneath his rock, looked for ways to cheat his opponent. When Stink was about to win, Satan sometimes commanded him to make bad moves that allowed Satan to double and triple jump, or reached his hand out to knock the players off the board. When Satan grew tired, he took Stink's ankle and held it clasped between his teeth while he slept so that his slave would not run away.

One night as they played checkers, Satan said, "Looking back, it's all been a bit of a disappointment, really."

"Sir?" asked Stink. He moved a checker with his long delicate hand.

"The whole thing. This, I mean. Hell. The Enemy returns to earth, he judges the living and dead, separates the goats from the sheep, and I take dominion over a billion new souls. I had been looking forward to it ever since my first triumph over Adam. There was even a time – just after a tragic underestimation of a certain little Jew-carpenter – that I had lived in terror that the Judgment itself was a trick in which I would lose everything. We spent a thousand years

getting the wording of the contract just right. I was a wreck
– it seemed as though everything had depended on those
souls, the sudden inpouring of new spirits and the
enfleshment of the old." He jumped one of Stink's pieces.

It was a bad move, because Stink double jumped and
made a king. "So?" said Stink. "It all came true, didn't it?"

"But there was no savour to it. Just more work.
Organization, tortures, expansion, construction – so much to
do. And for what? Without me overlooking every single
thing, there was rebellion, vandalism, disobedience, lack of
respect. As if they had a better place in mind, as if anyone
was forced to be here, as if they didn't choose it themselves!"
He had become quite angry, and he reached out a black-
nailed claw and batted the checkerboard away. "Let's play
again," he said, feeling a little better.

Stink retrieved the scattered checkers and set them up
again. "Not that I would have had it any other way," Satan
continued.   "Not that I would have done anything
differently." He moved a checker. "You know what my one
regret is?" he said. "That is, if I had any regrets? It was
allowing those sneaking spies in. I never thought the Enemy
would stoop so low." And while they played, he told Stink
the story.

Ages after the Second Coming, he had noticed that some
souls were missing. It had happened completely by accident:
he had taken a different route from the torture chambers to
his palace and passed through the main office. There were
three files on the desk, and a name he recognized: a Supreme
Court Justice who had been a loyal servant from the time he
had joined the bench, now condemned to have his flesh torn
with wire and skull crushed with forceps for all eternity.
Satan asked where the Justice was.

"He's not anywhere."

That was impossible. Of course he was, he was just hiding. Had they looked for him?

"We sent out five search parties. He's not anywhere."

Satan demanded that they find him. He slashed at one of the clerks with a long claw, opening his front from his throat down to his belly and spilling his stomach out.

Days later, the news came back: the Justice had left. There was a hole in the gate, and spies reported that the Justice had thrown himself at the feet of the Enemy and been accepted into Heaven.

Satan's stomach shook and his loins and buttocks turned to water. He grabbed the messenger and tore him in two. "How can this be?" he cried. "The condition was eternity! The law said eternity!" He stormed off into the deeps of his castle, where he blew into the forge until the fires turned bright as the sun. He lay down in the flames and stayed there for three days and three nights. How could God make things change in eternity?

"Ages ago, when we were still trying to escape this place ourselves, we had pointed out that any unit of time was infinite, since it was infinitely indivisible," Satan explained to Stink. "A minute has sixty seconds, but each second has ten one-tenths of a second, and each one-tenth of a second has ten one-hundredths, and so on so that even a single million millionth of second is an eternity. At first I thought that this was the answer."

"And it wasn't?" asked Stink.

"No," said Satan. And he told Stink about a saint he had tempted a thousand generations ago. Satan had mocked the Enemy's ridiculous claim of omnipotence. "Does God have the power to make a rock so big that he cannot move it?" Satan had asked. The saint looked at him. "Yes," he said. "And then He would pick it up."

News of the escapes flew to the furthest corners of Hell. The Supreme Court Justice, an auto mechanic who had killed his wife, and a United Nations diplomat – all had slipped over the frontier, begged forgiveness before the Judgment seat, and, after countless years of torture in Hell, been granted God's grace and mercy. Many in Hell were skeptical and made fun of the news, many jeered and laughed at the weak-kneed sinners who would rather be slaves of God than their own masters. But from that day forward, Satan's authority and power waned rapidly. When he was not present, his orders were not obeyed. When he appeared, he was not shown fear nor even deference until he made some display of power.

More of the damned left. A spy was discovered in one of the outlying provinces: an angel from Heaven named Abdiel, who was exhorting and preaching the Justice and Mercy of God to the masses of Hell. He was placed upon the rack, and nails were hammered into his hands and feet while the wheels pulled on his wrists and ankles. But they had no power over him, and he was released and escorted to the gate.

"There is no need for you to be here!" he shouted as they led him through the streets. "Turn away from your sin and be saved!"

Abdiel caused a sensation. Rebels rose up against Satan, he was openly mocked in the streets. Even the devils who had been with him from the time before Earth ignored his orders and precepts. Armies attacked his palaces and stole his booty. A bomb exploded in his bed one night, arrows and daggers and darts flew at him when he walked down the street, and his dinners were filled with poisons. Every day the roads swarmed with people and devils heading for the gates. Satan flew at them and bit them, he poured acid on them and threw up fogs and darkness, but still they came to the gates and splashed out of Hell into the river. His storerooms were looted and the evil old ferryman bribed with the treasures of all the ages. Rebels and insurgents attacked the palaces, the furnace workers left their forges, and the torturers freed their charges despite Satan's orders and punishments. To rest between battles, Satan began sleeping beneath the rock that would later become his home. Meanwhile, the towns and provinces of Hell emptied like an artery that had been cut. Even the ferryman left, and the refugees began swimming the great river. Soon Hell was empty but for Satan and Judas, who had sold God and man for thirty pieces of silver. Judas, at least, thought Satan, will not desert me. But one day Judas shook the dust from his feet and walked through the gates, and Satan was alone in Hell.

"Which reminds me," Satan said, "how do you happen to be here?"

Stink had backed Satan's last checker into a corner with his kings, so that Satan could only move one forward right, one back, one forward left, one back, and neither Satan nor Stink could win, and neither were they making exactly the same move three times in a row, so the game could not officially be called a draw. Stink pointed this out: "If you move the same way three times, the game ends in stalemate, but if you keep doing that, the game will go on forever."

"Not if you let me take your king," said Satan.

"Why would I let you take my king?" asked Stink.

"Because you are my slave," Satan said, and his black nails sticking out from the rock dug into the stones beside the checkerboard.

So Stink allowed Satan to take his king and win the game.

*

One day Stink announced that all the renovations and building Satan had commanded were completed, and Hell was once again as it should be. "Except for that rock you are lying under," said Stink, "I have transformed every inch of Hell."

Satan thanked his faithful slave. "Excellent!" he said. He was looking forward to a real palace again, to his blast furnaces and factories and dungeons and fortresses. "And what reward do you think you are owed?" he said suspiciously.

"Oh, sir," said Stink, a little uncertainly.

"Perhaps you think you should be my second-in-command," said Satan. "Or perhaps you would like to govern some region of the netherworld as my representative? Or would you like a particular department – tempting, tortures, border patrol, espionage, immigration, tourism? What do you want, Stink?" During his speech, Satan's voice changed several times, now insulting, now friendly, now threatening, now fatherly.

"I don't really know," said the slave, "but I think I would like..."

"Silence!" Satan commanded, and his voice rang out and the stones themselves trembled. He shot out a long arm and grabbed Stink by the throat, pulling him down so that his face was pressed into the rock. "You have no desires but my desires. You have no will but my will. Yet you scheme to betray me like the rest of them." He reached around so that his claw held the back of Stink's head by the hair. Still lying beneath his rock, he pulled Stink's head back with his long arm and slammed the face into the rock. "You think that I do not know your little game. You think that I do not suspect that you have already betrayed me once. I know where you have been," he said, slamming Stink's face into the rock again so that he could hear the sound of the cartilage in the nose cracking. "You were one of the betrayers who went to Heaven. But it wasn't much to your liking, was it? No! And soon, just like you, they'll all be back." For that is what Satan thought had happened. He pulled Stink's head down and pressed it into the gravel so that he could see his face from beneath his rock. Stink's eyes were black and swollen shut, and his nose was flat and bloody. Satan licked some of the blood. "You thought your work would win my favour. But I have no favourites. You live only for me. You exist only for me. Your body and soul are mine. You will be the first to suffer in the torture chambers you have built. That is your reward. And when I am in my new palace that you have built for me, I will look down on you in your agony, and my joy will be complete." He again bashed Stink's face into the rock, then let him go. Stink collapsed into the dirt. "You gave me wine when I asked for blood. Now I shall feast on your blood."

Stink lay on the ground beside Satan's rock. "Present your neck to me, so that I may satisfy my thirst." Satan said it quietly, but in a voice of such power he knew that he would be obeyed.

Stink groaned, but he lifted himself shakily to his elbows and crawled back so that his neck was beside Satan's mouth. Blood from his face speckled the rocks. "Give me your throat," commanded Satan in a hiss. Pushing himself heavily and panting, Stink rolled over so that the back of his neck was at the opening between the rock and ground. Satan bit into his throat, fastening his teeth around the thick jugular vein, and he sucked the pumping blood into his mouth.

He had not had blood since Judas Iscariot left. But this blood was not as he remembered it. The taste reminded him, not of horrors and power and fear and conquest, but something he had not thought of for a long time: his days in Heaven before all the battles began. He remembered the day of his Creation, his entry into the ineffable light of God's presence, and the unqualified joy he had felt. He remembered the choir and the stately dances of the angels, which he had once himself led for the glory of God, who made all things right and good. He began to wonder what he had been doing all these countless ages. How could he have spent all his time fighting, when all he had to do was give in, to admit that God was, after all, greater than him, and not his equal. Was that so hard? God had created him, not vice versa. Why not just assent. Why not?

He sucked on the sweet tasting blood from Stink's neck and began to eat the flesh and bones with mouthfuls of stones and rocks and gravel. Everyone else had left him, there were none to impress nor command here. Why not cross the river, fly to Heaven, beg forgiveness? He had taken such a long road to get back home. His eyes filled with tears as he thought of how hard his life had been. Harder than the life of any other being from Earth, Heaven, or Hell.

He finished the last morsels of Stink's flesh and lay beneath his rock sucking on a stone that had some sticky intestinal material on it. He resolved that he would positively make some effort to get up and leave his empty old kingdom. With that thought in mind, he fell asleep and dreamt of his life before Hell.

He awoke with a terrible headache and the uncomfortable memory that he had somewhere to go today. Then he remembered: he had been thinking of giving in. He immediately became angry with himself. A little blood had gone to his head. Then he remembered with pleasure that before he had eaten him, Stink had finished his grand renovation of Hell. He resolved to stand up and take a look around. Then he decided not to bother. Then he remembered that he had been toying with the idea of repentance, and his anger gave him the energy he needed so that he pushed the rock off his chest and stood up.

The quick motion of standing after lying down for so long caused the blood to rush to his feet and his head whirled. A dazzling light blinded his eyes, and he staggered and almost fell. Instead of furnaces and fires and smoke, there was a garden, there were flowers and trees and the sun and sweet smelling grasses. Except for the little hollow in which he had lain under his rock, Hell was gone. The earthly Paradise had spilled over into it and filled it up. Satan was so dizzy he sat down on his rock.

"Hello," said a voice he recognized. He looked up, and saw, standing above him, a man wearing Keds. But as he raised his eyes he realized that it was not a man at all, but a burning angel speaking to him. The angel's face was shining and kind, and his beauty was such that Satan was terrified and could not look at him, and he stared instead at the soft flowers on the ground beneath the angel's idiotic shoes. "Do not be afraid," said St Michael the Archangel. "There is still time." He smiled. "There is more than time. There is still all eternity." He reached down and held out his hand.

Satan did not take the hand right away. He began to cry. He looked up at St Michael, whose blood and flesh and bones had filled him and made him drunk. Standing whole above him, St Michael held out his hand. Satan stood and took a step forward. All around him the birds were singing, and in the distance he could hear the angel choirs and the great choir of all the dead, now joined together into one great chorus, singing to God in a voice that tore at Satan's stony heart. Why shouldn't he again join the choir? Why did he need to fight endlessly, to deny endlessly, endlessly to withhold, to contradict, to refuse? Why was he the one to be so sacrificed? To sacrifice himself? Looking into the beautiful face of the Archangel, Satan held up his hand.

He took a step forward, caught his toe on a stone and stumbled.

Satan screamed and turned around. He fell flat on the ground screaming, he pulled his hair and bit the stones beneath him. He rolled into the depression that his body had made in the ground. He pulled his rock over him so that his head was covered by the indent it had made over the centuries. There he lay for many an age, alone and in the dark, dreaming of the great kingdom of Hell that had once been his.

Above him all around the renovations of St Michael grew and flourished. The sun shone down and the angels sang, the lion and the lamb lay down together to nap beneath the stars, the saints wrote songs and stories, the horses and dogs played together in green fields of limitless beauty. But Satan did not see nor hear. He stopped his ears with sand, he put mud up his nose so he would not smell the flowers, he covered his eyes beneath his rock, and lay there, a single spot of Hell in the midst of Paradise.

How the Horse and the Dog Left Paradise
and Came to Serve Man

THIS STORY, LITTLE ANNE, begins before the world was as we know it today, in the days the when lions and sheep still played together in the forests, when the angels walked beneath trees to write the first books of science, when the clear blue rivers swam to the ocean in a slow dance. In the evenings the angels sat with Adam and Eve and taught them about our Lord, and then they sang together with the birds and the monkeys and all the choir of nature. For these were the days when Time was still the horizon of beauty and had not yet begun its slow inexorable destructions.

Of all the animals in the world, the two greatest friends were the dog and the horse. The dog was brown and white and black with floppy ears, a black nose and a happy grin and a long tongue. The horse was broad and sleek, and his shaggy hoofs were each as big as a fat raccoon and thundered when he ran. Together they would take long walks across the world, for in those days the oceans had not yet split the continents apart. The dog liked best to smell the good things God had made, the flowers, the leaves of the cedars, the warm rich earth. He was quick and high-spirited, and ran from tree to tree and flower to flower, smelling all the varieties of scent, now standing here to catch a new flower on the wind, now running there to mingle the smell of the earth with a patch of strawberries. Just as the painter mixes his colours on a palette, now adding a touch of blue, now a touch of yellow, so the dog mixed the smells of the world, now the honeysuckle, now catalpa, now roses (in those days, the roses had no thorns). Every day the dog would run about with his friend the horse.

The horse did not have as keen a sense of smell as the dog, but he loved the dog and loved to watch him run over the world. The horse was slow and strong and quiet, and on their long walks, he often wandered off to ponder the mysteries of God: of Time, which is bounded on all sides by Eternity; of the created world, which seems self-sufficient, but is entirely dependent on God's will for its existence at every moment; of the beautiful order of the universe, the perfection of God's creatures, rocks, hills, rivers, lakes, animals, man, angels. The horse was far-sighted, and had already divined that man, created in God's image, would have a special role to play.

"We must get to know the man and the woman better," said the horse.

"Yes, we must," said the dog.

"It is the man who will be the key to this," said the horse.

"The key to what?"

The horse was not sure. "I can't see yet what will come next. But the man will play the largest part."

"I'm sure you're right that we should know the man better," said the dog, "But I'm not so sure you need to be so mysterious about it." And he was off to a particularly sweet-smelling patch of lilies.

*

In the evenings the two friends curled up together to watch the stars and listen to the angels singing in the skies above them. Sometimes, in the distance, they would see the angels turning in great circles in their dance of praise. "Now there's a reason to get to know the man better," said the dog, resting his head on the horse's soft belly and looking up.

"Angels visit him all the time. I would love to see an angel up close."

The horse snorted and laughed. "That's only what you say when there's no chance of us meeting one any time soon. From a distance they're all just light and dancing and music. But up close, you'd be so scared you'd turn tail and run until you crossed seven forests and a field. The angels are powerful and important, and not for the likes of ordinary folk like you and me."

"I didn't say I wanted to do their business for them. I just want to see one some time. Have you ever met one?"

"Once," said the horse. "He was a very minor angel, not one of the Seraphim or Cherubim, and certainly not an Archangel at all.[1] I had a question I was thinking of, about how Love worked. I was lucky enough to happen on him when he was leaving the man."

"And were you scared?"

"Terrified," said the horse, and laughed. "He shone so brightly I could hardly see. He looked at me and said, 'You have a question.' I was so frightened I could hardly speak, and he told me not to worry, but only tell him what I wanted. And even though I had been thinking about the problem for weeks, I knew, seeing him there, that it was a stupid question really, but that I was a stupid creature and it was only as far as I could get without help. So I asked."

The dog rolled on his back in the grass and waited for the horse to continue, but the horse was looking up at the stars

---

[1] Angels, of course, have no sex, and cannot rightly be called 'he' or 'she'. This story uses the masculine pronoun because in those days the "he"s of the world were rather a better lot than they are today. Besides, it certainly doesn't seem right to call an angel "it", which is what you call a table or a rock. You could call an angel "she" if you liked, which would be just as inaccurate as "he", and I would have done so here, except that that isn't what the horse actually said. He was a boy horse.

and lost in thought. Finally the dog said, "Well, what happened?" and he poked the horse with a brown paw "He laughed at you, I suppose. Asking questions above your province."

The horse shook his mane and nodded. "Well, he did laugh at me. But it wasn't bad or cruel. I sort of had the feeling that it isn't really in the angels to laugh at us on our account – they're too serious, sort of a deep, happy seriousness, but too serious to laugh because someone is silly or stupid. It was a kind sort of laugh, like the question had an answer that was very obvious to him, but that he was pleased I had gotten far enough to ask it anyway. So he told me the answer, and asked me some questions that I had never thought of, and I remember it was very exciting and intimidating at the same time, all those questions he had for me. I wanted him to talk forever, he seemed so wise."

The two friends lay on the ground looking up at the stars. After a time the dog asked, "What did he say, exactly?"

"A lot of things," said the horse. "The simplest thing he said was that God was love." He stopped for a minute. Then he said, "But you know how it is with them. They don't *talk*, really, it's more direct, almost like talking to yourself."

"I don't know how it is, actually," said the dog, "because I've never had a question just when an angel happened by. But I would dearly love to see one up close sometime."

*

It happened that the next day the dog found some orchids, his favourite flower, at the edge of a great green wood. While he stopped and sniffed his fill, the two friends heard, coming from the heart of the forest, the sound of a huge deep voice singing. Because they had just been talking about angels, they decided that that was who must be making the music.

"Let's go and find him," said the dog.

"We've never been to this forest before," said the horse.

"All the more reason," said the dog, and he was off down a narrow trail and into the woods.

The trail they had started on soon disappeared, and they were forced to retrace their steps several times when the trees and bushes grew too closely together and would not let them pass. They thought that they must be in a very old part of the world, since they had never seen trees so tall and wide. The dog found many ancient flowers and fungi to smell, and the horse walked silently behind him, listening for the music they followed and pondering the ancient things of the earth. It was still morning, and the wood was strange and beautiful.

The music they heard was odd. At times it was lovely, but then it would quaver and dart and dive, as if the person singing was practising a difficult passage and not quite getting it. But angels, who are pure thought and will, do not need to practice, since there is no shadow between their ideas and the realization of them, as there is for you and me. Besides, the strange part of the song kept repeating like a refrain, so that it seemed impossible that it was just a mistake or practice.

"An eccentric angel, singing a new kind of song?" asked the dog.

The horse did not think so. "The thing about the angels's songs is that they are so *accessible*," he said. "Even when they're singing about things that are wise or deep or difficult, you always feel you understand when they sing. As if the music were a way to communicate things you couldn't just *say*. But this – what does it mean? It just sounds – I don't know what it sounds like."

"And you know all the songs of the angels, do you?" laughed the dog.

Just then the song was lovely again, and the horse began to feel foolish. "No, I suppose I don't. Perhaps it was just the echoes through these trees playing tricks on me." They agreed that it was a strange forest they were in, and perhaps the thick-grown trees and bushes and brush were affecting the sounds.

But as they walked, the strange passages in the music were repeated again and again, and even the dog had to admit that there was something in them that made his hair stand up. "What on earth could he be singing about?" So the friends continued on. The trees were now so high that they could not see up to the tops of them, and the light in the woods turned green and dim because of the canopy of leaves. They could hear the trees whispering to each other as they passed. The dog's tongue was hanging out of his mouth and the horse – who was really too large for such a thick forest – was puffing and blowing from the effort of pushing his way through the trees and bushes.

In those days, the air was so clear that sounds could be heard a very long way off, even the sound of someone singing in the distance. So it was almost night before they came to a clearing in the very heart of the woods, and there, under the red sky of the setting sun, they saw the snake.

*

Of all the animals in the garden, the snake was the one with the most beautiful voice. He was eloquent and clever, and he was always surrounded by friends, including the great builder, the spider, and the scorpion, with his tail that dripped a fragrant wine. For in those times, all the animals were beautiful, for God made all things good.

The scorpion was red and had armour like a lobster and sparkling black eyes. "It's the d-dog," said the scorpion. He stuttered a little when he spoke, at first glad to see the two friends, then less sure, as if worried what the others would think.

"And the horse," said the little brown spider in a sneer – but also looking over at the scorpion and the snake to see if he was supposed to be sneering.

"Hello," said each the dog and the horse, who were disappointed not to find an angel.

"Friends, friends!" cried the snake, and he stood up and walked over to them on his four legs – for in those times, snakes still walked like the other animals. He was a very pretty sort of snake, with blue and red diamonds and big yellow eyes with long lashes. "Please, come, sit down, welcome, welcome!" And he shook his head expansively, inviting them into the clearing, and rubbed against their sides in greeting. "How happy I am to see you. Why, we three were just talking about some of the cleverest and bravest of the animals, and of course, your names came up. Wonderful, wonderful," he said, and walked back to his place in the centre of the clearing.

The dog and the horse walked into the clearing and lay down. They had walked a long way and were tired and a little stiff, as they realized only when they sat in the cool grass. The scorpion and the spider, who had given them such a strange greeting, were now all smiles.

"We heard singing," said the dog, "and thought it might be an angel. But then there were strange parts in the music as well. Was he teaching you all something? A new song?"

The spider and scorpion looked to the snake, who laughed modestly. "Oh no, oh no," said the snake, almost to himself, chuckling and shaking his head. "Goodness, to be confused with an angel! Imagine," he said, and looked around. His friends chuckled as well. He continued. "No, unless you heard something from somewhere else, we've been here alone all week, haven't we?" said the snake, and the other animals concurred. "But we have been working on a new song. A new *kind* of song. Is it possible that you heard *us*? Although why you would think we sounded like angels..." and he chuckled and shook his head again, looking at the ground.

The dog and the horse were a little embarrassed too, since, when you actually see them, no one could confuse a snake with an angel, even a four-legged snake. "It did sound very beautiful," the dog said.

"The sound through the trees," said the horse. They did not want to make the snake feel foolish by comparing him to something so high above him, nor did they want him to feel as though they did not like his singing. And so they were relieved when the snake said,

"Would you like to hear the song we were working on?"

They agreed that they would like that very much.

"I have been working on this for some time now, and we three --" he indicated the spider and the scorpion, "-- have been practising it all day." And the three began to sing.

What they sang, in exactly the words and music, I do not know. In those days, music itself was better than it is now, and songs could go on for hours at a time in verses of dazzling beauty and complexity. The snake's song began like many of the songs heard in Eden in those days, as a psalm or a hymn in praise of the world and its beauty, and when the snake sang in his deep voice, joined by the other two – who had lovely voices as well – you could easily see how someone, at a long distance and through a great forest, might mistake their voices blending for the voice of an angel.

But as the song went on, it began to leave the established order of music and dipped and dived and thrashed about. The dog and the horse immediately recognized these passages as the strange sounds they had heard on their walk that made their hair stand up. Although the music and its words went by quickly, its subject had changed from the beauty of the world and the splendours of creation to the most important animals on earth and how unfair it was that they did not get more.[2]

When the music ended, the giant trees that surrounded the clearing were whispering to each other. The sun had now set, and only the smallest and most distant of stars could be seen above the clearing. The dog and the horse were both very uncomfortable, but the snake smiled at them and said, "Did you like it?"

"Ye-es," said the dog, but he was not sure.

"Some of it," said the horse. They were confused because they had never heard music that they did not like before, and so they were not sure what to say – just like the

---

[2] I know I am interrupting the story, but there is something you may not know. In those days, music was not only better than it is now. It was also more *accurate*. For instance, if I were humming a song about a tree, and you did not know the words or anything about the song at all, you would be able to guess the song was about a tree. A song about a sad thing *sounded* sad, and songs about happy things *sounded* happy. Which is why, when the snake's song turned to wicked things, the song itself sounded wicked and made the dog and the horse uncomfortable.

Music now is never as accurate as it used to be, which has to do with What the Snake Did Next and What Came of It, and also with a story about a Great Tower that men tried to build. But now I am getting ahead of our story. I promise not to interrupt it again.

first time you try a new kind of food, you may need more than one bite to figure out what you think.

"What don't you like about it?" said the snake, and he became very cross.

"Well," said the dog.

"Well," said the horse. They did not want to hurt the snake's feelings. But the horse, who was wiser, said, "There was the part where you started talking about the important animals. Was that all right?" Although he knew that he did not like that part, he had never not liked music before, and so he was not sure how to talk about it.

"You mean this part?" asked the snake, and he threw his red and blue head back and sang in his sweetest big voice about the important animals and how unfair the world was to them.

"Ye-es," said the dog, whose hair was standing on end.

"Ye-es," said the horse, who was trying to figure out why he didn't like it. "It just seems — wrong. Like it's not true, or a story someone made up. But a story that doesn't teach anyone anything, but only would make them feel bad." He was not sure he was saying what he thought exactly, but that was the best he could do.

"That's exactly it," said the dog, and while it wasn't exactly what he thought either, it was pretty close.

"You mean this part?" asked the snake, and he smiled at the horse and the dog with a sort of greenish smile, except that his yellow eyes were not smiling at all, only his teeth, which were long and pointed. And he sang the part again.

"Yes, exactly," said the dog.

"Yes, exactly," said the horse. "That was the part."

"Well," said the snake, and he hip-hopped back and forth on his four legs, "that just shows what you know."

"That shows what you know," sneered the brown spider, who was building a little castle out of some rocks.

"That is the new part that we are writing, and it is a new kind of music, music that has never been heard in Eden before," said the snake, and he seemed very angry. Then he became calm again, and he fluttered his long lashes over his big yellow eyes, and said the next part in a very soft, soothing voice (remember, he had a beautiful voice). "You just don't appreciate it because it is so new. You must remember that we're all musicians here," and he nodded at the spider and the scorpion, "and we know the secrets of music which estimable fellows like yourselves," he nodded to the dog and the horse, "really would be too busy to learn much about." And he talked about keys and notes and chords and harmony and structure and form, all in his deep beautiful voice and all of which is very interesting, and to be sure about which he knew a lot, and he sang examples to them from all kinds of songs, with the scorpion and the spider sometimes joining in. The dog and the horse were so interested in his talk that they had almost forgotten about the snake's new song. Until finally the snake said, "But that's all by way of background. What I have done with *my* song is to change the way music works. I have rewritten the rules to make something new."

"But what if the old way is the right way?" asked the dog.

The snake smiled, but again his eyes did not smile, only his teeth. "The old way," he said, "is only one way. It's just the way you happen to be *used* to. When you get used to *my* way, you'll like it even better. That's how it works."

"Still,..." said the dog.

"But,..." said the horse.

"I am not interessted in your ignorant opinionss," said the snake, who was now not pretending to be nice and so angry he was hissing on all his esses. "If you are not ready for what iss new, you can sstay with the old. I am not going to wasste any more time on the likess of you. I will take thiss new mussic to the man. He iss vissited by the angelss. He will understsand."

And the snake stomped off on his four feet. The spider stuck out his tongue and scuttled after the snake. The scorpion – who was a little embarrassed – said, "I guess we'll see you later," and then ran off too.

The dog and the horse were quiet for a long time. Then the dog said, "What was that all about?"

The horse did not know. They had never been involved in a fight before. "It certainly makes you feel bad, though. I wonder if we should talk to the man about this?"

The dog did not know why they would do that. "He doesn't need our help. He's much smarter than we are. Besides, we've been walking all day. I'm exhausted."

The horse, who had found it very difficult to push through the tangled brush, was even more tired than the dog, and he said, "I suppose the man and the woman can handle the snake." So they lay down in the clearing and fell asleep listening to the whispering trees and the distant songs of the angels in heaven, the old kind of music.

*

The next morning the horse woke when it was still dark, and he nudged the dog awake with his hoof. "We must find the man at once," he said. "I've just had a horrible dream about the man and the snake. He is in great danger." So the dog and the horse set off again through the great forest before it was light.

As they walked, the forest seemed taller and more whispery than ever, and every pathway seemed to disappear before them and force them to retrace their steps and look for another way around. The horse in particular – because he was so large and the brush in the forest was so dense and tangly – often had trouble pushing through snarls where the smaller and more agile dog could jump up or twist round or worm through. "The man, the man," the horse kept saying. "We must warn him." The horse decided that he was too slow and that the dog should go on ahead as fast as he could.

"But what will I tell him?" the dog asked.

"The snake, the song – tell him," said the horse, who was stuck between two trees and whose eyes were rolling.

I won't tell you about the rest of the trip through the forest – all the wrong turns, all the windings and detours that each of them had to take until they finally came back to land they recognized – or about the dog's hurrying so much that he didn't sniff a single flower, not even the orchids that he loved so well that lined the outside of the forest. Breathless and panting, his tongue hanging out the side of his head, the day was over and it was the next night when he found the man at the top of a tall hill. The man was squatting on the ground and tearing a small flowerbush up by its roots.

The dog ran over to the man and licked his feet and legs. "The snake," he puffed. "I have to warn you – the horse said – a new song – danger --"

"Leave me alone," said the man, and he shoved the dog so hard that the dog rolled over three times before he could get his legs under him.

"The dream – the horse said --" said the dog.

"Get out of here," yelled the man, and he picked up a stone and threw it at the dog.

The stone hit the dog on his hind leg, and he stumbled away. He was very frightened – he had never been hit by anyone before, and certainly not by someone he had admired as much as the man – but he came back, his tail pointing down between his legs and his head close to the ground. He said, "The horse said to tell you. The snake will come to you, and there is danger..."

The man snarled a laugh. "I've already talked to the snake. And there is no danger *at all.*" As he said the words 'at all' he jumped at the dog and kicked him as hard as he could.

This time the dog – who was so tired he could hardly stand – rolled all the way down the hill and landed in a heap at the bottom. He lay there panting. On the hill above him, the man had turned away. The snake had already come. He was wondering what to make of everything, when, from the other side of the hill, he heard the woman humming the snake's song, and then he knew.

*

There is another Book that tells what happened with the man and the snake and his music – how the snake found the woman first, and the woman listened too carefully to him, and then the man listened just as carefully, and they both were convinced and followed the snake's advice. Then the man and the woman were thrown out of Paradise and the snake lost his beautiful voice and could only hiss and he lost his legs and had to crawl in the dust. The snake's friend the spider began to build with webs that came out of his belly, and the scorpion's tail of sweet wine now drips poison. All God's earthly creatures – the trees and plants, the animals and fish, the stones, and man himself – fell because of what the man did. As they left Eden, each of the animals had to come forward in turn and stand before an angel of God, a member of the eternal burning seraphim, whose faces dart out fiery light. The dog and the horse waited together to stand before the angel.

"I always wanted to see an angel up close," said the dog.

"Now you get your wish," said his friend.

"But I never wanted it to be like this."

Then they were called forward.

"You are to be expelled from Paradise, and the curse of the snake and the man will be put on you," said the angel and there was a flame on his brow. "See what the future holds for you." And before their eyes, each the dog and the horse had a vision, the horse of fear and night, of being chased and pulled down by great cats and packs of wild animals whose eyes were glazed with the love of blood. And the dog saw wildness growing in himself, and his teeth grew longer and the muscles in his jaw hardened until they could crush bone, and he saw his mouth covered with blood, himself standing over a corpse and howling in the wilderness, and the dead body was his friend the horse. Both the dog and the horse were terrified.

"Great angel, do not let this happen," said the horse.

"Oh no," whimpered the dog. "Do not let this happen."

The angel looked down at the two friends, and his beard was a leaping fire. "What would you choose instead?" asked the angel.

The horse was wise and far-sighted, and he saw that misery was to come, but also a great hope. He remembered that they had heard the snake's song before the man heard it, but that they did not warn the man in time, who had made such an evil choice. And so, because he saw the man needed them, he said, "Let us serve the man, to help and guard him." And the angel was pleased with the horse and the dog, and he granted their wish.

*

And that is why, little Anne, when the animals were expelled from Paradise for the sins of the man and the woman, the horse and the dog left to go with the man and serve him. They do not have easy lives. The dog guards our houses and our sleep, and, because of the great love in his heart, plays with us and tries to please us. The dog's nose is not so keen as it once was, and he cannot smell flowers anymore, but he still uses his nose to identify his friends and to find things when they are lost. The horse spends all his days working, pulling carts and ploughs and carrying man on his back. The dog will fight for his master even if he will lose, for dogs are loyal and brave; and the horse will work for his master even when he is so tired he can hardly stand. Neither the horse nor the dog talk anymore, but only neigh and bark; and they are no longer friends, for when they left Paradise their love for each other was sundered, and they are estranged.

But men and women everywhere love the horse and the dog, because they help us in our need. None of the horse's wisdom was left to him, and he became one of the stupidest animals. But his wise choice served him well, and that is why we have dogs and horses to this day, and why men will have them until we all will be made wise again together, by the Second Coming of our Lord, at the End of Time.

The Devil's Confession

THE NIGHT BEFORE the oils had been blessed on the feast of the Last Supper. Today the organ did not play, and there was no cloth on the naked altar. All the statues were covered over in purple robes, since there would be no saints if Christ had remained dead on Good Friday. Five different readers read the story of the Passion. Then the entire congregation came forward to kiss the feet of the cross. There was no mass, since the bread of angels could not be consecrated on such an evil day, and the extra communion hosts from the night before were used. The altar of the Blessed Sacrament was left empty as a sign that Christ had died.

Now the second great feast of the Triduum was over and Fr John could relax until Easter Sunday morning. He slouched in the back pew drinking a glass of red wine and thinking of nothing. The church was dark, lit only by candles.

Fr John had the odd feeling that someone was looking at him. He shifted in his pew and looked around. Two burning eyes stared at him from beneath a tall purple ghost. Fr John started, then sat back. The cloak over the statue of St Michael was not long enough, and beneath it Lucifer was visible, beaten under the feet of the archangel. It was the glass eyes of the devil come alive in the candlelight that had startled Fr John.

"Thrones and dominations, principalities and powers! Hello, old Nick," said Fr John, who was in a good mood. He held up his glass in a toast to the statue.

The devil said nothing. The bottom of St Michael's spear was also visible beneath the wrap, sticking into the back of Satan.

"I suppose you thought you had won on this day two thousand years ago," said Fr John. "First you tricked man into driving a wedge between himself and God. And then – imagine – getting God's consubstantial co-equal *homoousean* Son to incarnate himself so that God himself became subject to your rule. Yes sir," he toasted the devil again, "You certainly had everything going your way."

The devil's eyes sparkled with fire, and seemed to fix Fr John with a stare, so that he began to feel uncomfortable and looked over his shoulder. I should not be drinking in the church, he thought, although he felt that the main thing wrong with it was that people would talk. The Blessed Sacrament had been removed to the Sacristy, so he was not even showing disrespect. Still, that was the kind of thing that was clear in the seminary and not so clear in parish life. He began to walk around the church and sat down next to the Virgin's altar. The statue of the Virgin was completely covered over in purple, even her feet. He looked back across the church to the statue of St Michael. The rows of candles in front of the archangel's altar gleamed in the devil's eyes, so that no matter where Fr John walked, the devil seemed to stare directly at him.

Outside a noisy April rain was shushing against the roof and down the windows of the church. Although the days were getting longer, the clouds had made this one dark early. Fr John got up and walked back to the statue of the devil. "In a way, it makes sense not to cover you over today," Fr John told the statue. "This is your day."

By all reckonings, Fr John was a happy priest. He was not even thirty-four years old and he had his own church.

The parish was reasonably well-off and stable. Unlike many of his older colleagues, he was comfortable with the casual way people took one another nowadays, so that he was not fazed when people came to church in jeans, or took God's name in vain, or when they lived together without being wed. At the same time, was able to make it clear that neither he nor the Church approved such things. He managed to be both orthodox and humourous, to hate the sin and love the sinner, so that the older parishioners looked on him as a dutiful son and the young people looked up to him as an older brother. He had been very successful in convincing people to stay and believe in the Church. Even his bishop liked him, because every year he managed to raise as much money as parishes much larger than his.

But Fr John was not all happy. Drinking was not his problem – although he recognized it could become one and was careful about it. Nor was lack of faith. In an age when so many could not even conceive of God, Fr John was blessed with a constant sure knowledge of his presence. His problem was the dreamlike quality of his life, the sense that nothing he did was important, that he was superfluous to the comfortable world around him. Everything had been so pleasant and easy that he felt as if he was missing something. He had spent a six months in a monastery where the old monks had spoken of life as the Way of the Cross: "Even as our Lord suffered for his flock, so every Christian suffers for Christ." But the Way of the Cross was not a Way Fr John was familiar with. Sometimes at night he felt the desire to find pain simply to remind himself that he was alive, and he would punch the doorframes in the rectory or bite his own shoulder as he lay in bed.

Fr John sighed and drank. "You lost," he told the devil. "Your greatest triumph became your most complete failure.

And your time is running out." He raised his glass to the devil, and drained it. The devil's burning eyes stared at the priest.

Then there was a banging outside the church, and one of the heavy front doors opening and slamming shut in the rain. Fr John jumped a little. He thought, I really am nervous today. Through an archway, he could see into the vestibule, where a stranger in trenchcoat and hat was stomping on the carpet and shaking out his umbrella. Fr John regretted that he had not locked the doors. He put his empty cup of wine behind the devil, and wondered if he stood quietly, perhaps the man would leave. After all, the church was officially closed.

The stranger did not leave. He stumbled over to the dishes where the holy water was usually kept and peered into them. They were empty, because there was now no holy water until Easter. Fr John took a quiet step behind the statue of the archangel to stay out of the stranger's line of sight. He felt giddy, like a child running away from a parent.

The stranger walked forward into the main part of the church, and Fr John realized he was not stumbling, but limping badly, as if one leg was shorter than the other or one foot did not work properly. With every step the stranger dropped, pivoted, then pushed forward so that his bad leg came forward in a semi-circular arc. What is a cripple doing out in the pouring rain coming to church an hour after the service is over? thought Fr John. He was angry that the man had a disability, since that made it more difficult to send him away. Still he stood behind the statue watching.

The stranger was now peering into the darkened church towards the front altar. He looked as if he could not decide whether to genuflect and come in or to leave, and he stood leaning heavily and dripping on one of the back pews. Since the Blessed Sacrament was not even in the church, Fr John decided that it was too much to let a lame man kneel down to nothing, and he stepped out from behind the statue. "Can I help you?" he asked in his coldest, most professional social worker's voice.

Now it was the stranger's turn to be startled, and he jumped a little as Fr John appeared from the side of the church. "Hello, father," he said.

"The Good Friday service is over," said Fr John. "I'm afraid you missed it." Although he had just been wandering aimlessly about the church, he had remembered some paperwork that had to be done. He wanted the stranger to leave.

"Oh, altogether all right, father, altogether all right," said the stranger in a mild accent that Fr John could not quite place. He stood smiling amiably.

"Well. Is there something I can do for you, then?" asked the priest.

"Why, yes, father, there is," said the stranger, speaking in his strange accent and smiling his friendly smile.

It seemed as though he was not going to say anything else, and so after what seemed like a long pause Fr John said, "What would you like me to do for you?"

The stranger smiled. "Hear my confession," he said.

Fr John felt a pang of fear, and he asked himself why he should be frightened. He said, "Confessions were from noon until three o'clock today, why do you come so late?"

The stranger just smiled. "Weren't those who started late in the day paid the same as those who were there from the beginning? I have heard," smiled the stranger, "that everyone is welcome, even those who were once lost."

Fr John wanted nothing to do with this man. He told himself that church was closed for the day. He told himself that he had paperwork to do. He told himself that this fellow could have come to confessions at the scheduled time like anyone else.

"It was Pilate who washed his hands rather than help one poor unimportant man," said the stranger.

Which is what Fr John had been thinking.

Fr John looked at the wet man and his bad leg, which, he noticed, had an oddly-shaped shoe at the end of it. He listened to the rain falling outside the church. How could he send this man home, who had come to him on such a day? "All right," he said. "Call to mind your sins. I have to get my stole."

The stranger smiled broadly, and his eyes gleamed in the candlelight, so that he reminded Fr John most of the statue of Satan he had been talking with just minutes before. It was at that moment that Fr John realized that he was not talking to a man at all, but a devil sent from hell.

Thousands of generations ago, when Adam ate the fruit of the tree and disobeyed God's law, God looked for a way to punish him. Satan came to God and begged that he and his devils be given the task. God, who knows all things in advance, gave Satan the power of death and allowed him to wield it against man as a punishment for man's sins. And so all men and women who sin are subject to Satan, and all the dead must pass through his kingdom.

But God loved man, and he did not leave him to be a slave to Satan forever. And so, in the fullness of time, God sent Christ as a man to earth, where Christ fell into Satan's power, as all men must. Satan killed Christ and took him to his kingdom in hell, which is the punishment for sin. Satan thought that he had won, because Christ did not open his mouth, he did not complain, he went quietly with Satan, as so many had done before. Satan thought that Christ went quietly because he too had sinned. So it was not until they arrived together in hell that Satan learned that he had no power over Christ, the Sinless One, and while Satan laughed and showed Christ all his treasures, his gold and jewels, the souls of children and babies and animals and trees and all the men and women of all ages, Christ struck him down and said, "Fool, you have broken your contract with God and with creation, you have taken a man without sin for yourself." And Christ ran through the tunnels of hell, gathering the souls that had been trapped there for long years and freeing them from the torments the devils had arranged for them. And the last thing he did was take from Satan the power of death, so that now only those who invite Satan into their hearts need fear him, but over those who follow the way of Christ Satan has no power.

The devil sat in the empty church pretending to pray, but really reciting the names of evil things under the earth to bolster his courage. His bad foot – the one that he had used to kick the archangel Michael before being thrown from heaven – hurt inside his wet, oddly-shaped leather shoe. Devils can see into the future darkly, so that they can never be sure of their predictions, but in council in hell they had all agreed that Fr John would one day become a powerful force for their Enemy. The usual temptations seemed not be working – for although devils can see easily into the hearts of the sinful, the hearts of the just are hidden from them. And they could barely see Fr John's heart at all.

And so, in council, the devils decided on the most dangerous plan they knew. They would tempt Fr John to eternal despair by confessing their sins to him. For no man can hear the sins of a devil without breaking his heart and forgetting all the goodness of God, the sins of the devils are so black. And besides breaking the spirit of Fr John, the council of devils had a deeper plan.

"We know," said Beelzebub, fat as a pig and slimy as a fish, "that Christ tricked our great father, Satan, and stole his power."

The other devils nodded and complained, they drooled on the stone council table.

"Likewise," said Beelzebub, waving a long-nailed finger in the air, "we will steal the power of grace from God. In the confessional, the confessor receives grace, through the priest of the Enemy's church. The one of us who receives this grace will bring it back here, to our dark furnaces beneath the earth, where we can learn its secret, the secret power of God, and turn it back upon God Himself."

Cards were drawn, and one of the devils took the low card, and he was sent to earth to tempt the priest in the confessional.

The devil knelt reciting the names of evil things. Besides the pain in his foot, he was also nervous. Devils avoid priests and churches and holy places as a matter of their own comfort, because Godly things burn their flesh and confuse their hearts. But on Good Friday the body of Christ was taken out of his church, the holy water was drained from its basins, and all the terrifying statues of the saints were covered over with drapery. The devils felt sure that if their plan could be accomplished, it would be on a Good Friday, when the churches were sad and unprotected. Besides, the devil who had come was young, as devils measure these things, and confident in his strength. He felt sure he was stronger than any priest. He hoped to break the priest's spirit before the terrible words of absolution were spoken, the words that called down the power of God to forgive all sins. In that case, he would not receive the power of grace to take to hell, but he might at least destroy the priest. In case the priest was strong enough to withstand even the horror of the devil's sins, the devil held a stone in his pocket, which he would place in his mouth when the priest said the words of absolution over him, so that he would not cry out during the prayer.

For his part, Fr John was also frightened, but he could not refuse the request of a sinner for confession. While he put on his surplice, soutane, and stole, he listened to the devil muttering the prayers which were really curses, and he shuddered. He thought of stopping his ears with cotton or candle wax, but he could not find anything the right size, and besides, a priest ought not to give absolution for sins he has not heard.

Finally Fr John was ready. The two went to the confessional booth at the back of the church, the priest sitting in his centre area and the devil kneeling in the stall beside him. The priest slid the wooden door open, revealing the dark amiable face of the stranger behind the metal grate. "Bless me father, for I have sinned," said the devil. "These are my sins."

The devil began to relate his sins to Fr John, and there was no end to them. Beginning from before the earth began, when he first turned against God and bit the heel of the archangel Raphael, to his tricks in the Garden of Eden, through the cruelties of animals and men and women through all time down to the present, he recited his sins, and there was no end to them. The strange and horrible sins pierced Fr John like cold knives, he slipped from his chair and knelt on the floor in his little box, he swayed back and forth, he placed his burning forehead against the tile floor to cool it. He wanted to cry out to God to stop the torment,

but his tongue stuck in his throat and he could not speak.
The devil continued on, and slowly his man's voice with its
strange accent thickened and deepened until it came to
resemble the deep black-hearted thunder. Fr John looked up
and saw that the aspect of the devil's manhood had fallen
from him, and his burning eyes glowed like fire through the
grate, and his face was black and his teeth were fangs and
spittle hung from them. The storm outside increased, the
sun set and darkness filled the church, but still the awful list
of sins continued, for there was no end to them.

Mabelline Crory was already old at the time this
happened. She was a holy woman, who sometimes saw
angels in the sky, and when she prayed she swayed back and
forth in the ecstasy of her communion with God. Many of
the people in the church did not like her. Some thought her
visions belonged to another age a long time gone, and they
did not want the church to be medieval and old-fashioned.
Others did not like her because her visions were confusing
and inexplicable, and they seemed too modern, as if the
church were not the old church of Christ but some New Age
invention.

On the afternoon of Holy Saturday she came to church,
but found the doors locked against her. On the way she had
met a man raking the dead leaves in his garden. He told her
that a horrible red light had appeared in his windows, and
that the neighbours had seen fire and burning, others had
heard the sound of horrible laughter or witches' voices.
Then he laughed and said, "That was quite a storm, the
lightning was so bright and the wind howled so loudly."

Mabelline Crory waited for the church to open, but it did
not, and she went to the rectory to see if there was a mass
that day, but the rectory was also locked and quiet. Perhaps

Fr John has gone away until Easter Sunday, she thought, and there is no mass. She went back to the church to look in the window and see if Fr John was there but had only forgotten to unlock the doors. But although the day was bright and fine, there was no light in the church, and she could see nothing but darkness through the window. Then she heard a terrible noise from inside the church, and she crossed herself and said a prayer for Fr John, then went back home to wait for Sunday.

Inside the church the sun seemed never to rise. Fr John wanted to cry out and stop the devil, but his voice was too weak and he could utter no sound. Outside the darkness had lifted, the sun rose, but still the devil talked on, reciting even more horrible and bloody sins, so that he talked on all through the day and the people passing by the church shook their heads and talked about the awful noise coming out of the church, as if some insane organist were playing at full volume, or a choir of idiots were all screeching at once. The sun set and darkness fell again, and Fr John lay bathed in sweat on the tile floor of his booth, while the devil leered above him and poured out his sins, as if the entire flood of Noah were raining down upon the priest's head. The devil's deep voice had become hoarse as the roar of the ocean, he had talked from Friday afternoon until Saturday night.

Finally, he stopped. Whether he had actually finished the list of his sins, or if he had forgotten the rest, or if he had just grown tired, he stopped. The silence hung in the air like the purest moonlight. The devil looked down through the grate and saw Fr John lying huddled on the floor as if he were dead. For a second, he felt pity for the priest, who had heard more horrors than ever living man has heard. Have I killed him, then? he thought. He looked around him at the wooden confessional, he felt his knees stiff on their kneeler. He felt in his pocket for the stone he had thought to put in his mouth. He dropped the stone on the floor and listened to the harsh echoes in the empty church.

Suddenly he heard a sound next to him. The priest had lifted his head from the floor. The devil stared down at him, and almost smiled.

"For these, and all the sins of your past life, I now absolve you," the priest whispered. "In the name of the Father, ..."

The devil began to scream.

The sun rose on Easter Sunday morning and the faithful made their way to church. The bells rang, the organ played, the hymns were punctuated with Alleluias, and the Gloria was heard for the first time since Lent had begun. All the statues were uncovered so that the saints could witness the glorious day of their Lord's triumph. The altar was wrapped in purest white, and the burning Easter candle stood beside the Lectern.

No one recognized the priest who celebrated the mass. Mabelline Crory thought that perhaps Fr John was sick and had gone away. The new priest was the opposite of Fr John in almost every respect. Where Fr John was young and strong, the new priest was old and stooped when he walked. Where Fr John had been quick and chatty, the new priest moved slowly and spoke softly. Where Fr John had been happy and, perhaps, overly optimistic, as if he had not seen much of life, the new priest conveyed the impression of an unbearable grief, as if he had seen more of life than anyone should. He made Mabelline Crory think of a child who has just learned for the first time that there is evil in the world, or a young man who has been robbed of both his money and ideals by a swindler.

When it came time for the new priest to preach his sermon, he began to speak of the great sadness of God, who created all things beautiful and good, and the ingratitude of a creation that forgets Him and chases all manner of foolish things. "And it is on Easter Sunday that our betrayal of God is the greatest," he said. "For we do not have to sin anymore, because Christ has freed us from sin. And yet," he said, and he looked around the church sadly, "and yet." He paused. "But this is not an occasion for sadness," he said, as if trying to convince himself to be happy, "because Christ rises again, He gives Himself to make us strong, and we can start all over again, and God's heart can yet be made happy if only we listen to Him."

The sermon ended and the mass continued with the unhappy new priest. It was not until they took the communion bread from his hands, and he looked into their eyes and said to each of them in turn, "The body of Christ," that they realized that this was their Fr John Viator, now old before his time and sadder than any man they had ever seen – for Fr John had heard all the sins of the devil, and broken his heart. But no one in the congregation knew. One by one they came and took the body of Christ and one by one they recognized their priest.

The mass ended and the people left the church. Some stood about at the back hoping that Fr John would come down so they could ask him what had made him so old, what had happened that made him so sad. Some thought that his parents must have died, or that he had been diagnosed with a cancer since they had seen him last. He came down and walked past them, but no one asked him any question, they all fell back before him, the saddest man they had ever seen. They only said, "Hello father," or "Thank you, father."

"Hello," said the priest.   "Thank you all.   A happy Easter." His voice was hoarse, and he walked with a slight listing to one side, as if his foot bothered him. He walked out of the church and into the little house next door, where he lived.

"He walks as if his heart has been broken," said an old man standing next to Mabelline Crory.

Fr John would live many years after this happened. He went to Africa on a mission and found many converts eager to listen to the gospel and to be baptized into Christ's own church. He came back to America and preached in churches from Mexico City to Yellowknife and St John's, and everyone who heard him found something in his words that spoke to them, because Fr John understood the sins of all men and women. He visited schools and prisons, the rich and the poor, the wise and the foolish, and touched them all. He lived a life of poverty and obedience to God, and he could never forget all the sins that he had heard, nor his broken heart. He offered God his sadness and the gift was accepted.

But that was all to come in the future. On that Easter day, the sun was shining, and the parishioners walked out into a beautiful Sunday afternoon. The smell of new life growing was in the air, and the first tulips lined the street with colour. The thunderstorms had turned the grass from brown to green. Above them in the heavens, the angels sang the happy songs of God's praise. The angels see the glory of God all the time, they do not lose sight of it like man does, and they are always full of wonder and never bored nor tired. Mabelline Crory, with the body and blood of Christ inside her, could faintly hear the angels sing, could faintly see their many-winged forms in the air above her. The angels dipped and soared, they danced in great flying wheels for the glory of God, they sang in voices strong as the ocean. And among the angel host she caught sight of its newest and happiest member, the fallen angel who had repented, the devil who had confessed his sins to God's priest on earth, Fr John Viator, who took away his sins and gave him in their place the grace of God our Father in heaven, who loves all his creatures, even those who have sinned and fallen away.

III.   GRACELESS TALES

THERE WAS A MAN who put all his faith in his wife. He depended on her for everything, and although they fought and he beat her, he loved her more than himself. When she went away he was filled with jealousy and a rage he could not control. One day they took him to prison and when he came back, his house had burned and his wife was gone. The only thing left in the house was a charred and dusty note on the floor. The note said, "Mary – Gone to the grocer's. Back soon. B." It was in his wife's handwriting.

He asked everyone he met whether they had seen Beatrice. Many people had seen her, but no one knew where she was. Some had not seen her for years. Some spoke of her as if she were long dead. Others seemed to think they had seen her more recently, but none could say where. They sent Malley to neighbours and relatives and to graveyards. Some people had recently lost loved ones to disease or old age and wanted to talk to Malley about their dead. He was not interested in them. "All I want to know," he would say, "is have you seen Beatrice?"

Malley travelled as far as Dublin and wrote to people asking for word. Most of her family were dead, and the ones who were not lived in Canada and had not seen her for years. He stopped in every grocery store and talked to every Mary he met. Was the letter to Mary McGrath, with whom he had gone to school? But she had died of influenza. Could it be Maria Hogan? He did not know who the Mary in the letter might be. He wrote a letter to Mary Carruthers, who read the news on the radio, but she never answered. He looked at Beatrice's letter so often that the pencil faded and the words disappeared.

Mr McNulty, who had been a friend of his father's, gave him a job as a bartender. When he kept annoying the customers with questions about Beatrice, he was moved to the back to do stock. He began to drink when he should have been working, and Mr McNulty had to let him go. "I tried to do right by your father, boy," he said, "but I can't have you doing that."

"Where is my wife?" Malley asked.

"You won't find her at the end of a bottle," said Mr McNulty.

Malley began to stay at home and drink. He lived with the Browns, who had been kind to his wife and would sometimes talk with him about her. Then he would sit in his apartment with a bottle of whiskey and sing ballads and marches:

> By the old Moulmein Pagoda,
> Lookin' eastward at the sea
> There's a Burma girl a-settin'
> And I know she thinks o' me.

"He has a lovely voice," said Mrs Brown to the neighbours. "But he's a bit off, you know."

With some encouragement and a word from the Browns to Mr McNulty, he began to sing at the tavern. Because he spent all his money on drink, Mr McNulty paid the Browns a small stipend directly, and told Malley he was working for tips and drinks people might buy him. That arrangement worked well until Malley found out that the Browns were taking his money. "It's worse than the penal laws," he shouted. "Just because I'm Catholic you won't pay me? You're stealing my money just as you stole my wife." He began to shout filthy words, and Mr Brown had to hit him and push him out the door. Even while he shouted and Mr Brown hit him, Malley found himself watching the whole scene from outside himself, as if he had nothing to do with it. He noticed childish things: Mr Brown had a new mole on his chin, Mrs Brown had one eye slightly lower than the other.

He slept in a soup kitchen that night, then came back to the Browns. "I'm sorry," he said. "I'll collect my things and go."

"Perhaps that would be best," said Mr Brown. His new mole seemed to have grown in the night.

Malley moved into a back room at Mr McNulty's tavern, "Just until I get my feet on the ground." He told Mr McNulty that he realized many people had done him a good turn and that he had been ungrateful but he had been through a hard time and things would be different now. Malley was surprised that he said those things, since he did not know what they meant. He thought it was interesting that you could say things and other people would look at you and nod like Mr McNulty. He tried to discover what he did think, but he could not tell.

He sang in the bar that evening and people bought him drinks until closing. He told them about his wife, and someone said they had been talking to relatives in Toronto who mentioned a Betty Malley. A few hours later Malley broke open Mr McNulty's strongbox with a crowbar and left on a freighter for Canada.

In Halifax he stayed with a family of Biodans who thought he might be a relation, since Mr Biodan's grandmother had been a Malley. Malley talked about his wife at dinner. Mrs Biodan asked, "Did you know any Biodans in Ulster, Mr Malley?"

"The Biodans in Ulster! Of course I know them."

"Oh, how lovely!" said Mrs Biodan.

Malley intended to tell them that the Biodans were doing very well, there was a new grandchild he had heard, and perhaps the younger boy had been elected mayor. He began by saying some of these things, but then the story started to get away from him. He told how Mr Biodan had been in jail overnight, just for a little argument at a bar, you see, a very little argument and after all, boys will be boys, you shouldn't say a thing like that about a man's wife, but you know, boys will be boys. And how they must have thought Mr Biodan was dead, because when he came home his wife was entertaining another man, but he came back and found her, found her in the arms of her adulterous lover, and he threw acid on them and threw them out and then set the fire, and the name of the man, the name of the man who had done these things, what was his name?

Even as Malley was telling the story he could see that his story was not pleasing Mr Biodan, and Mrs Biodan had taken the children and left the room, but Malley wanted to hear the end of the story. He began to wonder where the story had come from and what it might mean, since he had never been to Ulster and did not know any Biodans there, but it all seemed very real to him when he told it. The next day he boarded a train to Toronto.

He met Mary Dornan on the train the next day, who had taught his wife geometry in high school. She was going to Saint Catharines to see her relatives, who owned a farm. "It's apple blossom time in the spring," she said.

They ate lunch together and sat in the cafe car while the train waited in Quebec City. She asked him about what he had been doing, but he did not want to remember the prison. It had been all people looking at you and fighting and looking at other people on television. The fighting was the only good part, but Malley was a small man and he had

lost more fights than he had won. Malley asked if Mary
Dornan had seen his wife during the last five years. He told
her that Beatrice had written to him about a Mary.

"It wasn't me she was talking about," Mary Dornan said.
"You know, it's a common name. Our Lord's mother."

The way she denied it made Malley think it was her, and
he asked again.

"I just told you, no. She isn't on board here with you, is
she?" said Mary Dornan, looking past his face towards the
snack bar as if Beatrice might be standing there. "Did the
two of you just have a little fight, now?" she asked.

Malley started to become angry. He had fought in prison,
he would not fight with Beatrice. He opened his wallet and
took out the paper. He took her arm and insisted that she
tell him where Beatrice was. "Look there," he said, holding
it up to her face. "Look there. 'Mary – I've gone to the
grocer's'. She was expecting you. Where is she? What did
you do to her?"

Under the pale yellow lights, there seemed to be no words
printed on the paper at all. Malley stared at it, then at Mary
Dornan's face. She had forgotten how to speak. "I – I – I –"
was all she said. Malley shook her arm.

In the back of his mind, Malley felt as if he were watching
the scene from a long way off, and he said to himself, "I
certainly have frightened her." But he continued to shake
her. "Where is she?" He thought, "Perhaps I should throw
her onto the tracks." He began to speak to her in
obscenities.

Mary Dornan began to cry and shriek. "Leave me alone!
Don't touch me!"

Suddenly two arms with brown hands were holding
Malley. He let Mary Dornan go. He began to struggle but
the arms holding him were very strong. He stopped. "Oh,

hello," he said. When the arms felt him go quiet, they let go. He turned around and stood facing a wide black porter. "Oh hello," he said. "This woman and I," he indicated Mary Dornan, "were just discussing the whereabouts of my wife, Beatrice, who seems to have gotten lost. She was suggesting that I come to Saint Catharines to look for her there, but I have informed Mrs Dornan that I cannot go, I have an appointment in Toronto. The train began to rock and I was worried that one of us would slip and fall, but it appears my intentions have been misconstrued, and ladies, women's liberation aside, are delicate. They are thinking of permitting them in combat now, I know, which I think is only their due, on a volunteer basis of course. Choice for everyone, an excellent policy, freedom, the foundation of the new world. Well, perhaps it would be best if I got back to my berth, or perhaps the smoking car, terrible habit I know, but so difficult to break." He began to walk away from the porter and Mary Dornan, but the porter followed him to the next car and watched him all the way down to the next. "Good-bye," Malley said. "Good-bye. The train doesn't feel so rocky now, I think I'll be fine."

Malley sat in the smoking car and stared out the window. There were trees everywhere in this country, trees and rocks and lakes and huge black crows. Closer to the train were telephone poles, and another track. The day was sunny and bright, but there was a quality in the light that was unfamiliar. I am ten thousand miles away from home, he thought, on the other side of the ocean. He thought:

> Then fare thee well my only love,
> Oh fare thee well a while,
> And I will come again my love
> Though 'twere ten thousand mile.

The train smelled of old carpets, smoke, and stale air-conditioned air.

Malley began to watch the other track so that the cross ties blurred and disappeared altogether with the speed of the train. His eyes stopped moving and he stopped blinking and became hypnotized. While he stared, he tried to think of Beatrice but found that he could not remember her. The man in the front of his mind continued to stare placidly out the window while the man in the back of his mind searched for Beatrice. The man in the back of his mind became agitated and violent.

*

"Are we having Mr Malley over for dinner?" Joanne Burns asked her mother.

"What's that, dear?" Mrs Burns was hard of hearing and the tap was running.

"Nothing," said Joanne. She scrubbed the potatoes and pierced them with a fork. She did not want to appear too eager. Her stomach was making noises already, although she had eaten three doughnuts after she had come home from work. Uncontrollable desires for food washed over Joanne so that no matter which diet she tried, she always broke it and had to start a new one. Joanne had wide hips and a flat chest and flesh hung from her arms like the arms of an old woman.

"I love a baked potato," said her mother, as she said every day when Joanne washed the potatoes. Joanne's mother was full of sayings that came out all the time. She would say, "Live and let live," or "It takes all kinds to make the world," or "Variety is the spice of life," or "A lady doesn't do those sorts of things." These old-fashioned sayings of her mother were the chief reason Joanne never brought any of her friends home. Her friends all called their parents by their first names. They smoked and drank and even swore in front of their parents. Joanne's mother thought her daughter was ashamed of their house, which was shabby and ill-kept since her father had died. "Your grandfather was the president of a bank," she would say, "You have nothing to be ashamed of."

Joanne's father had died when Joanne was still in high school. She had to work through university to support herself and used that as an excuse not to go out. "Are you staying in again tonight?" her mother would ask.

"I'm too tired to go out."

"Too tired? How can you be too tired? You're young, you should be out dancing!"

But Joanne did not want to stand at the pubs and watch her more sophisticated, thinner friends while she stood alone waiting for a boy to ask her to dance. Once, in a fit of bitterness, she told her mother everything: they were poor, she was ugly, all the boys drank and expected too much from a girl nowadays, and that her mother was too old-fashioned. Her mother comforted her. Then she said, "It takes all kinds to make the world. Variety is the spice of life. Besides, you have nothing to be ashamed of. Your grandfather was the president of a bank."

After university, Joanne got a good job in the accounting department of a large corporation. She started at $35,500, and there was talk of her mother selling the house and buying something smaller and perhaps Joanne getting an apartment of her own. Then the recession came and the housing prices plummeted, and Joanne was laid off. Now she worked as a secretary and made less than $25,000 and could not afford to move out. Besides that, her mother was older and a VON nurse came to visit twice a week while Joanne was at work.

Then one night six months ago Mr Malley came to the house. He was a handsome Irishman who had lost his wife in a fire and was a distant relation of theirs, but only by marriage, not blood. "Beatrice was my mother-in-law's aunt's girl," said Joanne's mother. She found an old black-and-white picture of Beatrice as a child from a wedding that had taken place in Cork. "At least, I think that's Beatrice," said Mrs Burns. Mr Malley asked if he could keep the picture.

Once, when her mother was in the bathroom, Mr Malley told Joanne how lucky she was to be young: "For one such as I, life is already over. There is nothing left for me to lose. But for you – endless possibility." His Irish accent was lilting and soft and he smelled of a deodorant soap. Joanne felt sympathetic bubbles flowing through her and she began to think about saving Mr Malley.

Mr Malley sang Irish songs and told stories. Although he was sad, he made Joanne and her mother laugh. Sometimes, when Joanne's mother said one of her sayings too often, or when she didn't hear something that was said, Mr Malley would look at Joanne and wink. The first time it happened Joanne's face got hot because it seemed that Mr Malley was making fun of her mother. But over the weeks Mr Malley became a regular part of their lives and she began to enjoy it, so that her toes curled in her shoes and her stomach felt giddy. Sometimes things from the house disappeared after Mr Malley's visits – an ashtray, a clock, money from the dresser – something Joanne noticed and, she believed, her mother did not. Once, while her mother was cooking in the kitchen, she saw Mr Malley slipping money out of her mother's purse into his pocket. He looked up and saw her.

They stared at each other for a second. Then Mr Malley winked. Joanne felt the heat wash up over her face. She turned and went back to the kitchen, but said nothing to her mother. She felt as though she and Mr Malley were allied in some special way that no one else could share, not even her mother.

Joanne and her mother ate their dinner and cleared off the table. Mrs Burns began laughing, and said, "Oh the stories that Mr Malley tells." Joanne felt a twinge in her stomach. She had taken biology in university and she knew that her feelings were caused by endorphins in her brain, but she always felt them in parts of her body. She began to wonder how an endorphin caused love.

The two women turned on the television to their favourite show, an American drama about the problems of beautiful millionaires. One of the millionaire families had taken in a beautiful poor girl for the summer. "I don't think Megan should stay out at night with that Billy," said Mrs Burns.

"Oh mother," said Joanne.

"I know, I'm old-fashioned," said her mother.

"She's so poor, this might be her only chance for happiness."

"She should wait till she gets married. If he can get the milk without paying the milkman, why pay?"

"Oh mother," said Joanne. "Things aren't like they were when you were a girl." As she watched the television, Joanne felt her dinner settling in her stomach and a dull burning splashing up around her heart. She shifted in her seat but could not get comfortable. She seemed so fat and ugly compared to the beautiful women on television. It seemed to her that there were two kinds of people – the beautiful and everyone else – and that those beautiful people lived in a different world from hers, where all the rules were different.

There was a rhythmic knock on the door and Mr Malley came in. "No, no girls, don't get up, it's only me," he said. "Perhaps I'll just help myself to a drink..." He went into the kitchen. Joanne felt the acid around her heart pulsing with anxiety and love. She was pleased at least that she had bought beer, which they kept on hand solely for Mr Malley's visits. It was not until he came into the living room that the women noticed the ugly scrape on the side of his head.

"Oh my gosh!"

"Mr Malley!"

With much fussing and rushing about, Mr Malley was sat down, cleaned and bandaged. He had many cuts and bruises, and his clothes were torn. At first he said he had only fallen. Then it came out he had been in a fight. He had been beaten by a Vietnamese street gang. Then he said it had been a British spy tracking him from Ireland because of his time in the IRA.

"Why did you come here?" asked Mrs Burns, who was upset by all the excitement. She did not want the British to attack their house.

"Mother!" cried Joanne. "Mr Malley is hurt!"

It was decided that Mr Malley would stay with them that night. The women tended his wounds while he drank beer and watched the television. Mrs Burns made him a hamburger.

Late that night, Joanne heard Mr Malley moving about downstairs. Her mother was snoring. Joanne put a robe over her flannel gown and went quietly down the stairs.

Mr Malley was sitting on the couch smoking a cigarette.

"Hello," said Joanne. She sat down on her mother's rocking chair.

"Hello." They sat together for a few minutes across from each other in the darkness. Joanne was sorry she had come. She was acutely aware of her dishevelled hair, which she felt falling against her scalp. Her breath was foul with sleep in her mouth and her flesh sagged in her loose nightgown. Then Mr Malley said, "You are very beautiful."

Joanne looked down and felt the blood heat her face. "You're making fun of me," she said. She wished she were back upstairs in bed.

"You are not like other women. They are all realistic and calculating, while you are shy and uncertain, like an innocent little girl." The words sounded beautiful in his accent. He took her hand and brushed his lips across it.

"Mr Malley," said Joanne. She felt pressures and gases rising inside her and travelling up and down, from her intestines through her stomach to her lungs.

"Please – I am only John, you are only Joanne, when we are together." He moved forward to embrace her, but the sudden motion awoke his wounds and he winced.

"You're not well," said Joanne, taking his arm to soothe him.

He was suddenly annoyed, and he pushed her away and stood up. "I must go," he said. "Now that I have been found, I must leave tomorrow night. I love you. I will stop here to take you with me."

He went out the front door. Joanne stood in the cool darkness and watched him disappear up the street. The street lights were shining and a milky-silver glow hovered on the sidewalks. A car passed. Joanne did not know what to think. Was he making fun of her? She felt herself blushing, and closed the door. How could she leave her mother and go off with a man who was wanted by the police? She walked up the staircase and climbed into her cold bed. She wanted to examine everything rationally, coolly, but her mind kept wandering. She thought of her mother, of her father, of the people she had known at university, and she argued with them in her mind about Mr Malley. When she finally fell asleep, she had resolved nothing.

At the office the next day, Joanne could not concentrate on her work. Her shoes seemed to cut her feet, the coffee and danish bloated her stomach, and she had to go to the bathroom all the time. Her fingers made mistakes at the keyboard and she forgot to run the spell-checking program. She pressed the wrong keys on her computer and made the system crash, so that no one could work on the computer until they fixed it. She forgot an important letter that had to go out, and Mr Rabinowicz, her boss, yelled at her. When she had taken the job as a secretary, she had thought she was underemployed. Now it seemed that even being a secretary was too much for her.

She went to the hairdresser's at lunch, but could not make up her mind about Mr Malley. How could she go with him? She had a job and her mother, she had her student loan payments. Mr Malley was wanted by the British police. But why did the police beat him up, why didn't they just arrest him and take him to England for a trial? Joanne's father had spoken of the IRA as heroes and freedom fighters, but Joanne had never paid attention, that was the old country and everything was different there. The IRA hated the British, who had taken over part of Ireland, the north part. She wished her father was still alive so she could ask him. Her mother would know less than she did. Was Mr Malley in the IRA?

Joanne had no taste for politics and began to think of Mr Malley. How handsome and dashing he was, how calmly he had come to their house after almost being killed in the

street. His wife had disappeared in a fire and now he
roamed the earth searching for her. Probably his wife was
dead, she had burned to death and there was nothing left of
her. She thought he needed to hear that from someone, that
he was carrying around this burden of his wife because he
could not accept that she was dead. She pictured herself
saying it to him: 'Your wife died in that fire. She's dead.
You have to move on.' He might break down, or swear, or
throw things at her, but she would be firm. 'She's dead.
You have to move on,' she would say again. Then he might
cry and she would comfort him. He would cry like a baby
on her breast. She imagined herself telling him it was all
right. She imagined them married and living happily
together. In her dream, she saw them together in a small
house in East York. They would be sitting down to watch
television after dinner, or perhaps Mr Malley would be
smoking a cigarette while she cleaned the house. Their life
together seemed perfect.

Then Joanne saw the other Mrs Malley, Beatrice, her skin
burnt and horrible and her clothes in flames, bursting
through the door...

Joanne paid the hairdresser and went back to work.
There was a new stack of letters to be typed in her in-basket.
Somehow she got through them and the day ended. She was
so anxious about Mr Malley that she could not think about
anything at all. On the way home, she stopped at a
restaurant and had french fries and a milkshake.

She felt numb at home all evening. Her stomach hurt
and she ate and ate to calm it.

Her mother asked her if she wasn't going to watch
television.

She didn't think so. "I brought some paperwork home from the office," she said. "I think I'll stay in my room and do it."

"I like your hair," said her mother, but Joanne was too guilty and nervous to say anything. She went upstairs. She filled a bag with clothes, then emptied it and put the clothes away, then filled it again. She realized she had no money and cursed herself. I must go to the bank machine right away, she thought. Then she laughed at herself, a cruel laugh, and thought, he was surely lying, he had been hit on the head and did not know what he was saying, when he comes again he will have forgotten he ever said it, it was the shock. Then she thought, but what if he wasn't lying, oughtn't she to have money if they were to run away? She went into her mother's room and took the last good jewelry they owned: a pearl necklace and earrings, and a diamond ring that had belonged to her grandmother.

"It's on," called her mother.

Joanne gave up her packing and went downstairs to watch television. Two of the beautiful Americans were getting a divorce. They argued and fought, then fell into bed together, then argued and fought. As Joanne compared herself to them, she realized how stupid she was being. This could not be her life. What would Mr Malley want with an ugly girl like her? But then she thought that No, this could be her life, she had only to take courage and seize her chance at happiness. When the show was over she ran upstairs to put on makeup and strapped her complaining stomach into an old girdle of her mother's. She fussed with her hair and sprayed perfume in it. She checked her bag again and hid it under her bed. She wrote a quick note and held it folded in her hand. Then she lay down to wait until her mother went to sleep.

*

One autumn morning Joanne went to work, came home, and went to bed. The next day she was gone. She had left a crumpled note in the bed: "Dear Mom – I've gone with Mr Malley. He loves me. I love you. Joanne." Her mother's first reaction was a mild anger, of the sort she felt when Joanne worked late and forgot to call. She'll be back, she thought, and she pictured herself saying it to someone, knowingly, as if because she said it, it must be true. But there was no one to say it to.

Then the sexual possibilities of Mr Malley together with her daughter hit her, and she began to feel it in her stomach and had to sit down. He's a widower, she thought. He's a travelling man. He's a musician. She thought of the horrible things men could do to women, how violent they could be, the strange things they wanted, the pain you could get. Even her poor husband, a good gentle God-fearing man, sometimes he was so different when the passion was on him. She sat on the bed thinking, Oh my poor poor Joanne. She thought of Joanne as a young girl, eight or ten years old, telling her how handsome Fred Astaire was. "Do you have a crush on Fred Astaire," Mrs Burns had asked, and Joanne blushed until even her ponytails seemed to turn pink. How different being with a man is from watching the beautiful Fred Astaire.

Then that was too much to think of for her daughter, and she closed off the room in her mind where those thoughts stayed and locked the door on them. But the feeling of them stayed with her, like the feeling she had that her husband was dead, and it spread through her body as though she had grown a little older and a little weaker. She looked outside, where the leaves on the maple had grown old too and turned red and yellow, like fire.

On the second day she called the police, but they could not do anything because Joanne had left a note saying where she was going. "It's not illegal for a twenty-eight year-old woman to leave home," they told her. They investigated Mr Malley but could not find anything about him.

"Do you know where he worked, or where he lived?" they asked her, but she knew nothing. She was full of reproaches for herself and her daughter: how could they have let a man into the house and never found out where he lived or worked? But that had been part of Mr Malley's charm, that he was always full of stories and songs and never talked about all those things, work or houses or taxes, that people didn't need to remember anyway. He had been like a holiday in himself.

The days went by and it began to rain and rain. Still Joanne did not come back nor phone. Mr Rabinowicz, Joanne's boss, called to see where she was. Mrs Burns explained the situation to him at length: her daughter had run away with a no good man, she was not that kind of a girl at all, she didn't know what she was doing. She kept talking until Mr Rabinowicz had to stop her and answer another call. He told her he was sympathetic but had heard nothing and could do nothing. He promised to call if Joanne turned up.

The rain continued and the leaves turned brown and thin and collected on the sewer grates. Mrs Burns called the neighbours, Mr Rabinowicz, the police. No one knew anything, they would call if they did. She remembered that Mr Malley had mentioned the IRA, which made the police interested again. They sent a Mountie in a business suit to see her, but nothing came of it. She continued to call until one day a policeman asked whether she had ever considered that her daughter might have wanted to get away from her.

The first snow flurries came. Mrs Burns went to the bank and discovered that most of the money had been taken out. Some cheques had been cashed and two draws had been made from bank machines. All this had happened out of town. At first Mrs Burns was happy because it was a communication from her daughter, proof that she still existed. But as she thought of it, she became furious, because Mr Malley was stealing their money. He didn't have a penny to his name, she thought, and now he's taking all our money. She did not close the bank account, however, and even made sure that some money from her social insurance went into it every month. Sometimes she watched the account balance dwindle and thought of Joanne using the money, perhaps to buy a new hat or groceries, or an iron or some flowers for the table, and she felt a happy kind of loss, as though her girl were growing up and leaving her but that was the natural order of things. After Joanne had been gone two months there was greying snow everywhere, but the withdrawals stopped.

When Joanne had been gone ten weeks Mr Rabinowicz sent Mrs Burns a cheque for work that Joanne had already done plus sick days and vacation days left. Mrs Burns wrote him a long thank you note in which she described her daughter and what she had been like as a child and about her crush on Fred Astaire, but she never received an answer.

Although she had been old and bed-ridden with Joanne at home, Mrs Burns found herself able to do more and more. Things that Joanne had done for years she now began to do for herself. She made tea and dinners. She began to go to the supermarket. One clear cold day the boy who delivered the groceries was sick, so she bought a bundle buggy and took them home herself. The nurse stopped coming. She said, "Mrs Burns, you're so healthy you'll outlive us all."

She busied herself with the practical affairs of running her house. It took her a long time to do simple chores. "The old grey mare ain't what she used to be," she told the house, but the work kept her mind off her troubles. She scrubbed the bathrooms every week and waxed the hardwoods the second Friday of every month so that the house shone. She began to go to mass every morning, except when it was icy, and she asked the Lord's mother for the safe return of her daughter. Sometimes at dinner she guessed wrong and made enough food for two and then thought of her daughter and cried.

Money was in short supply without Joanne's paycheque. A nephew she rarely saw came and moved her bed downstairs, and she closed off the upstairs to save on heat. She bought inexpensive foods like cream of wheat and peanut butter, pasta, frozen lemonade and bread and hot dogs and ground beef. She sold Joanne's car to the mailman for $1,200. There were no good clothes to buy for Joanne, no car insurance nor parking to pay, but still her savings were being used up.

After she had lived by herself five months the days grew longer and warmer and she took a part time job running a cash register at a fast food restaurant. At first she was quite frightened, but her boss was a nice young man named Tom who always let her go to the bathroom when she needed to and referred to her as a 'girl' so that she had to smile. Tom had kind eyes and a loud laugh and Mrs Burns found herself thinking what a pity it was that Joanne was not around, since Tom was just the sort of nice young man she ought to meet. The young boys and girls who worked there called her "Granny Burns" and she tried to give them an example of how to behave and pass on the things she had learned in life. "Live and let live," she would tell them when they argued, or "It takes all kinds to make the world," when the customers were unpleasant.

When the hot weather came, she was glad to work because of the air-conditioning. She took a little money she had saved and began to advertise for her daughter in the newspapers. She met another runaway girl named Joan through one of the ads. Joan was younger than Joanne and would have been prettier, except that she looked low class and hard. She wore dungarees and an A shirt so tight that her nipples showed. Mrs Burns thought: She looks as if she has seen and done too much. Joan was nice at first but then became foul-mouthed and began to demand money.

"I know you've got it — you old bitch!" she said.

They were in a coffee shop and the proprietor threw Joan out and then watched so that Mrs Burns could leave safely. Mrs Burns was happy to think that at least her Joanne would never act like that.

She went to psychics who asked her questions about her daughter and promised that she was all right, that she was in Ohio now, or New Mexico, or Ireland. One told her that Joanne had gotten away from the man who kidnapped her and found another love and they were married and lived in British Columbia, and that she was only waiting until Mrs Burns forgave her in her most secret heart, and then she would come home to take Mrs Burns to live with her and her husband and — yes, it was true, she saw this so clearly — Mrs Burns' beautiful new granddaughter. She had only to forgive Joanne completely, in her secret heart.

Mrs Burns did not want to believe the beautiful story, but she did not want not to believe it, and her heart ached at the thought that she had not completely forgiven her daughter.

"Forgive and forget," she had always said, but she began to wonder if she knew what forgiveness even meant, if it meant forgetting or promising not to be angry or something else. She went to confession and talked to the priest about her sins and whether or not she had forgiven her daughter, but the priest was soft and gentle and would not stay focused on the problem of forgiveness. She realized as she left that she had gone to confession because of the psychic, and since consulting psychics was a great sin in itself, she felt very guilty and had to go to confession again.

Three years passed. The humid summer days came again and Mrs Burns began to forget things and gave customers too much change, or no change, or gave them the wrong order so that they complained and everything was unpleasant. One day after she had given the wrong change to three customers in a row Tom told her to take the rest of the day off in an angry voice that made her frightened. She went home and phoned in that she was quitting. Later that week her nephew called to see how she was doing, and she told him she wanted to sell the house and move to the nursing home. She explained that her daughter had run away years ago, but that she might come back, and she must explain the story to the people buying the house so that they could tell her daughter where she was. She explained this to her nephew and the real estate agent and the people who came to the open house, until the real estate agent took her away. She did not like the real estate agent, but the house sold anyway. "It takes all kinds to make the world," she admitted to her nephew. The leaves had turned and the rain come when they took her to the nursing home.

If Mrs Burns ever found out what happened to her daughter, no one has ever heard. Not a day went by when she did not think of her, but she did not know what to think. Sometimes she thought that Joanne had gotten sick of her and run away and never wanted to see her again. Sometimes she thought that Mr Malley had kidnapped her daughter and was dragging her through dirty seacoast towns. Sometimes she thought her daughter was dead. She remembered a song Mr Malley had sung about a woman who was true to her seafaring love "though he's been gone for seven years." She thought of herself as the true woman and Joanne as the shipwrecked sailor who loved her but was lost at sea.

She did not have a television in her room, and sometimes while she waited for dinner she would sit and stare out the window at the apartment building across the lane. Then she would think that she had never thought her life would turn out this way, and wonder how she had thought her life would turn out. Sometimes tears rolled down her face while she sat and she forgot to move until the sun set and she looked up to find herself in a dark room and dinner was over. She would think, "Oh, Jennie, you're a silly old thing." Then she would go down to the common room to sit in a rocking chair in front of the television, where she watched the beautiful people and hoped for her daughter's safe return.

St. Christopher, Now Presumed a Legend

CORINNE MCQUEEN LIKED to think of herself as an investigative journalist. That was her official title, and it was printed on her business card. Her father called her a reporter, as if all she did were hang around parliament all day waiting for a quote, or he called her a TV star, as if she were just a pretty face that knew nothing.

Corinne was interviewing the mother of a five year-old boy who had kidnapped her son two and a half years earlier. The boy was fat and sullen and did nothing, it seemed, but watch television and eat junk food every day of his life. His mother had been moving every few months, from trailer park to motel to apartment to townhouse, from town to town, picking up waitressing or domestic or daycare jobs here and there, using fake identification to collect whatever welfare or childcare benefits she could. Her name was Mad. She was pretty but haggard, with circles under her eyes that would never go away. They sat inside her rented trailer on an old couch. The cameraman was set up in the kitchen.

"What do you do with Jeremy when you're out working?" Corinne asked.

"I leave him," said Mad.

Corinne pushed: "And that's all right? I mean, he's only five years old, and you leave him for an entire shift? Alone for eight hours?" She wondered if the woman would cry.

She did not. She was a thin slip of a woman and her eyes shone like a fish in a Disney cartoon and the muscles in her jaw pulled tight and she said, "He's five years old. He can take care of himself."

The big luminous eyes in front of a statement like that were a great moment, and Corinne was thankful that Mad had agreed to the television camera. Then she spoiled it, or so Corinne thought: she smiled sadly and touched Corinne's arm and said, "I leave him juice and food and he likes the teevee. I told him to go outside if there's a fire. I can't very well ask someone to look in on him, now can I?" And then she looked sadly off, a great look, almost as good as the big wet eye look a minute before. This was as good as it got, Corinne thought: the callous mother and the tender mother. She could use either one, or both, depending on how the father played.

Before she ever met Mad and Jeremy, Corinne was sipping coffee in her office and looking at the paper. She had been reading the personal ads and thinking about doing a sexy piece – some beefcake and a fashion model type and their adventures. The segment would be called "Rendezvous: Classified", a play on 'classified' ad and 'classified' top secret. She did not know she was on to something when she read Don's advertisement:

> Mad: I don't want to take him away, I only want to see
> him again. Can't we work this out? Don.

and a telephone number from out of town. It had been a good week, but the next month looked slow, so she dialed the number. It was better than she hoped. She made the appointment, and a week later took a camera out to interview Don.

His hair was closely cut around his head but then grew long from the ends down to his shoulders, the civilized animal look like rock stars wore in 1995 – no doubt his high school years. He had a moustache and the firm body of a working man in his mid-thirties. If not for his eyes that were too small and too deeply set in his brow, he would have been handsome. He worked at a union job in a refinery across the river. He was divorced and remarried. He had been awarded custody of his son by two judges at two levels of court. His ex-wife had disappeared and taken the child with her. That was more than two years ago. The boy was now five. He had tried the police, private detectives, he had contacted runaway homes, hospitals, orphanages, women's shelters.

Corinne stopped him right there. "Women's shelters? Did you beat her?" she asked. She was certainly not going to do a sympathetic piece on a wife-beater.

"I swear to God I did not," he said, and his voice even shook a little. He had never hit her. She drank. When he hid their money, she sold things – their television set, the car he had bought her. "Can you believe it? The car! She sold the car for 700 dollars while I was at work one day." When she couldn't get money any other way, she stole beer or bottles of vanilla extract from the supermarket. They fought, but he never hit her. "Would the judges have given me Jeremy if I hit her? God." He had married her out of high school, but it was a mistake. All she wanted to do was drink and read romance novels. When Jeremy came along, she got a little better, but it didn't last and then it was too late. When he was awarded custody, she stole the boy.

The police looked, but they lost interest when the case could not be closed quickly. He hired detectives who found nothing. Then he had no more money to spare. He had a new wife and new children. He ran advertisements for Jeremy in the classified ads when he had something extra – the three paycheque months, he said. "Maybe she'll see the ads and call me," he said. "I want Jeremy to meet his new little brother and sister." His tiny eyes blinked and blinked like a hurt animal.

Corinne planned to do three or four spots: first the documentary piece on Don, then Don's plea, short, simple, touching. Mad might come – many did when TV was involved – but if she didn't, there were plenty of detectives, and she had the budget to succeed where Don failed. When they found Mad, they would sit on the story for a week and run Don's plea again, to build it up. Then – boom! – the next week, a big announcement that Mad had been found, here's the boy.

Corinne had a sudden thought: What if the mother refused to be on the show? She put the thought aside. Two judges had given the boy to his father. If the mother didn't cooperate, they could always put a camera in the police car.

After the show with the family reunited, she'd let it go for a year and then do a followup. That would allow her to use the best stuff from the first shows and add the rest: a happy child reintegrated with his father's family – hopefully, of course. Or, a biased and patriarchal justice system stealing children from their mothers. Either way. The mother was a kidnapper, but Don was not as innocent as he wanted to appear. It was clear to Corinne that he had been involved with his new wife before Mad had left him.

It occurred to her that she might not be there a year from now if she could move up to one of the big networks before then. She had heard that some of the big journalists – Barbara Walters, George Will – owned the stories they contributed to their shows. If she moved, perhaps she could take the story with her.

The first time she ran only the father's plea: her voice-over setting up the situation with sad Kenny G type music and pictures of the little boy – not quite three years old in Don's photographs – and family dissolving into one another.

Then to the father, who ended with, "Mad, I just want to see my little son again."

The spot was a hit. They got almost three-hundred calls and letters from people who said they knew something. Corinne used the usual detective agency to screen them and follow up on the ones that sounded promising. Less than six weeks after she ran the spot she found Mad.

"I've been expecting your call," Mad told her when she made the first contact. "My son and I saw Don on TV. Of course, Jeremy doesn't know it's about him."

They set up a time to meet. "No cameras," said Mad.

"You can tell your side of the story," said Corinne.

"No cameras."

They met for the first time at a McDonald's on the QEW. The boy, small-eyed like his father, blinked and blinked in the sunlit parking lot and began to cry. When the mother and boy first came in, Corinne told them to go away, she was waiting for someone.

"For me," said the woman. "I'm Elizabeth – that is, I'm Mad. And this is Jeremy."

Corinne could not believe that a five year-old boy could be so big and fat – she would have guessed he was eight or nine. Jeremy clung to his mother's legs and began to cry, so that Mad said, "Excuse me," and went to order food with her blubbering son. She walked back to the table with him still clinging to her legs and crying. "Hush, Jeremy, hush," said his mother. As soon as she put the food in front of him, he hushed and began to eat. He did not look at anything but the food. "He'll be good now," said Mad, regarding her son fondly. "Jeremy doesn't get out too much.

It makes him nervous." She ran her hand through his hair. "He's a great kid, really." She lit a cigarette.

They sat and talked for an hour. She had been young and immature, she didn't drink anymore, she had been on the wagon for a year, she went to church and AA meetings when she could, it was all for Jeremy, whom she referred to as "the child." His father was cold and not interested in the boy, he said, 'Are you sure he's mine?' and other things.

Jeremy sat with his head down and ate his french fries. When they were all eaten, he stared at the empty container and began to cry. "Oh Jeremy," said Mad. To Corinne she said, "It's a phase." Corinne, who had no children, nodded. Mad walked to the counter to get some more while Jeremy held her and cried. Then she gave him the new fries and he put his head down and ate quietly.

Corinne pushed one last time for Mad to appear on camera. If she liked, they could film her in a dark room, or block out her face electronically, like that woman the Kennedy boy raped.

"Do you really think he raped her?" Mad asked.

"Oh honey, of *course* he did," said Corinne. "You want to tell your side. A single mom, hunted by the police. You think the judges aren't swayed? Why not appear? Everyone has pictures of you already – your husband hands them out. And no one can tell where you are by a TV shot..."

Jeremy ran out of french fries again and began to cry.

They agreed that Corinne would phone again and Mad would think about it.

A week later, Corinne and her cameraman were filming Mad in her rented trailer. Mad was pretty and reasonable. She loved her son, and that's what this was about. The judges had no right to take a boy from a mother who loved him. Corinne liked Mad.

Near the end of the interview, while they were drinking coffee, Corinne asked if she could bring the father to see his son and film it. Mad started as if she had just found a spider in her cup.

"I was just thinking that if you reconciled, you wouldn't be..." said Corinne.

Mad interrupted. "He's my son too. You can't take him away from me. You have no right. The judges have no right..." She spoke angrily on and on while Corinne said, "Oh, of course, of course."

"It was just a thought," said Corinne.

Mad looked at her suspiciously, as if something had just occurred to her. "You're going to leave us alone, aren't you?" she asked.

Corinne looked surprised and hurt. "No, no, oh no," she said, meaning Yes, she would leave them alone. "I wouldn't do anything I didn't clear with you first," she said. And she patted Mad's arm, to make her feel better.

When the interview was all over and they were in the car, the cameraman said, "Poor fat little kid. That woman should be shot."

That made up Corinne's mind.

The next day she made a deal with the police. She would tell them where the kidnapper was on two conditions: first, that they bring the father along on the arrest – "For the sake of the child," she told them. Second, that she be allowed to bring cameras.

Corinne decided not to run the Mad interview until after the raid, when she could splice the whole thing together – talking to Mad, the police, the boy. To run Mad first and the police a week later would imply that she had informed on Mad, that she was not herself on the side of freedom. But she was on the side of freedom. Of course she also was on the side of law and order. Sometimes it was hard to balance the two. Still, if she put the Mad interview together with the police raid, she could turn it whichever way worked out better.

A few days after she put the police on notice, she got a call from the detective agency: Mad was moving again. Corinne had her secretary get the plane ticket for Don and called the police herself. "We've got to move," she told them. She had the cameraman film her making the call, just in case.

The night was outside a small motel off Route 52. The motel was shaped like an upper case L, with the office at the top. "Free HBO Vacancy" said the sign at the front. "Wayside Motel" said another sign. The rush of the highway overlaid the constant chirping of crickets. An eighteen wheel Purdue truck dominated the parking lot. There were three other cars, one of them missing the wheels and up on cinder blocks. And Mad's old rusty Dodge Omni was parked in front of one of the doors.

Inside the office was a fat hairy man in shorts and an A shirt that did not quite cover his stomach when he stood erect. He was watching television and drinking red wine from a juice glass.

"What can I do..." he started to say to Corinne, and then the police came in. They described Mad briefly and mentioned her car, and the hotel man gave them a room key and number. Corinne was impressed by the contempt the policemen showed the hotel manager: minutes before they were laughing and joking about a baseball player who had lost a testicle, and now they were stony-faced and hard. They did not even look back when the hotel manager asked fearfully if there would be any shooting. Corinne wished she could be so cold – but, before she could stop herself, she turned back and said, "Oh, I don't think so, nothing like that," and smiled.

All the while, Don sat in the Channel Twelve car. He had not spoken the whole drive out, especially since the cameraman (who was also driving) was talking non-stop about a computer he had just purchased and all the things it could do. To Corinne it seemed Don was so tense he might have a stroke before they reached the hotel. She told him not to worry, they would have time to edit the piece and he should just be himself: "Just do what comes naturally and we'll get it on film."

*

Don sat in the car waiting. The police and Corinne McQueen herself had asked him to wait, so he did. He was sure that he was doing the right thing. Two judges had given him custody of Jeremy. The police were helping him. Corinne McQueen herself was taking a real interest in the case. The law was one thing, but a respected TV show as well – it just makes all the difference, Don thought. For two years – almost half of Jeremy's life – he had got nowhere. He admitted to himself that he was disoriented by the power he had unleashed: judges, the police, TV.

Now he sat in the car and watched. He was so nervous about the police and Corinne McQueen and the cameras that he could not imagine what might happen next. "Just be yourself, we'll take care of it," Corinne – she told him to call her Corinne – said. She had so many questions for him:

what was Mad like, how did she behave in this situation, in that situation, what sort of baby was Jeremy, what sort of toddler. She tape-recorded all his answers, filmed them, made notes, checked again for clarification. He had been on television three times with his ad for Jeremy, plus the original interview. He told all his friends, of course, but even people he had not told shook his hand and wished him well. Although he had stated he was now happily remarried and had new children, he had also had a number of propositions from various females – some of them very sexy. He was glad that Corinne had not pushed him on the matter of when he had married his second wife.

"Why don't you leave the boy alone?" Don's father had said. "He's been with his mother for more than two years. How can you take him away from his mother?"

But Don knew that he was right. He would not call it love – the songs about love did not describe his longing – but in some channel of his body flowed an unforgiving desire for his first-born son, flesh of his flesh, bone of his bone. He felt the fierce possessiveness of some wild cat for its young. Even if Mad had been good and wise, he would have fought for Jeremy in court. Though he put away religion the year he had discovered girls, the feeling he had for the boy sometimes welled up from his guts in the form of incoherent prayers, though to what or to whom he could not say. He found he had almost begun to believe in God again, simply because the idea that he no longer had any connexion with his son was too horrible to be true.

But now the time draws near. He stares out the car window. The police are talking through the motel door, one of them is fiddling with the key. Corinne McQueen is standing well back, the cameraman is hovering about, the powerful light on his camera staring at the door like an oncoming freight train. The police and someone inside are arguing through the door. Then suddenly the police are kicking the door open, their guns are drawn, one disappears inside and Don hears Mad screaming obscenities, and the sound of a young boy – Jeremy, he recognizes some quality in the sound – crying in a high-pitched wail. He looks for the car door handle, cannot find it, fumbles, tears a fingernail against the lever that opens the window, and finally, like release from a nightmare, the door is open and he falls out of the car to the pavement. "Where's the gun, where's the gun?" a policeman is shouting outside the door. Inside Mad is still shouting, Jeremy still wailing, and Don gets up and runs toward the room. As he runs, he calls "Jeremy, it's daddy, Jeremy," and he is blinded by the spotlight as the cameraman turns to aim at him. "Fuck you, fuck you!" Mad's voice screams into his blindness. Don comes to the door of the room and now his back is to the spotlight, but a large policeman bars his way. "Step back, back," says the policeman. He hears himself shout at the policeman, "That's my son, God damn it!" and the policeman moves into him and Don has to give ground. Mad is still shrieking, and Jeremy wails in fear as if wolves were attacking.

And then it was over. Mad subsided into soft weeping. "She didn't have a gun," said one of the policemen. Through the door Don could see Mad's backside and arms twisted behind her back and wrists handcuffed. "Oh oh oh," she wept in quiet despair.

Jeremy, held up by one of the policemen, appeared in the door, fat, blinking, dazed, crying. "I want mama," he said, trying to turn away from his captor. Don rushed to him and he flinched away. "Mama!" he screamed in his high-pitched voice, altered but recognizable as the infant Don had known for two years, now two years ago. "Mama!" He tried to sit down but the policeman held him up. "Mama! Oh mama, mama, mama," he said in little gasps as he cried.

"Jeremy!" said Don.

The boy lifted his tiny wet eyes to look at the stranger who knew his name. "Mama!" he cried, turning away.

Don took the boy's hand firmly in his own and the policeman let Jeremy's arm go. "I'm your daddy," said Don, and his voice choked him and water rushed to his eyes. "I'm daddy," he said, recovering himself, telling himself he must be strong for his son, but Jeremy was sitting down and pulling back towards the hotel room.

"Mama, mama!" he said.

Don pulled him towards the car. "That's all right, now, that's all right," he said. "I'm daddy. Daddy, Jeremy. I'm..."

"My daddy's dead," said Jeremy. His breath came in the short inhalations of weeping. "I want to see mama." When he said mama, he began to cry again.

Don pulled him toward the car. Corinne McQueen was walking with them pointing her microphone. The light, now in front of them, dazzled and blinded Don. A car engine groaned. Behind him, Mad's curses and weeping floated in the night. A policeman's voice was saying something to her – perhaps reading her rights.

"My daddy's dead. I want mama," said the boy.

"I'm not dead, Jeremy," said Don. He realized that with the light in his face he had missed the car. Corinne stood in front of him with her microphone pointing at them like a gun. He had a sudden urge to punch her face.

"Mama!"

Corinne was offering him something. He was about to scream at her, to tell her to leave them alone, when he saw what she was offering: a chocolate bar. He took it from her and gave it to Jeremy. "Here. Candy," he said.

"My daddy's dead," said Jeremy, looking up at Don and taking the candy. "Mama said daddy died a long time ago, and we had to leave."

"I'm your daddy," said Don. "And you have a brother and a sister, and there's a new mama too, and I am the daddy, your daddy..." His voice failed him.

"I want mama," said Jeremy. Still breathing in gasps and blinking away tears and the light, he began to eat the chocolate bar and allowed himself to be put in the car.

*

Jeremy was seven years old when Corinne McQueen met him again to do her followup report. His father and stepmother said that he had had many problems at first. He was frightened of everyone for almost a year, but the therapy had done wonders, and then of course the return to a normal life was probably the most important thing, living in the same place, seeing the same people every day, having brothers and sisters and parents and a routine. They had to admit, they owed it all to Corinne.

Mad could not argue that Jeremy was worse off. But she denied he was better off. "If the police hadn't hounded me, I would've done as well or better for my son," she said. But this time, she looked hard, with hair that had been puffed too much and eyes that never smiled. She had lost a brutality suit against the police for the night they had taken Jeremy away. She had been in and out of detox a several times since then. There was nothing appealing about her segment this time, unless it was her single-minded and pathetic conviction that she was right: "He's my son. They can't take him from his mother. I don't think it's right to take a child from his mother."

At the age of seven, Jeremy was a slim boy of medium height who weighed less than he had when he was five years old and fat. He had a B average in school and liked science and math best. After school he played baseball with the hardware store team, second base like Chase Utley. He stood his ground and fielded a slow grounder on two hops, but his throw to first was late and the batter was safe. "Charge it, Jeremy, charge it!" the coach yelled.

After the game, Corinne asked him some questions. "I don't see my other mom much. I think sometimes she talks to judges and people and then I'm not supposed to see her," he said. "But I remember everything. All the hotels were the same. I don't know who I like better. My mom and dad told me I don't have to decide, that they love me and that my other mom loves me too, and I don't have to pick because they all love me. So that's all right."

"Do you feel like you have to choose between them?" Corinne asked.

Jeremy sat and stared at the baseball diamond. It was empty now. A lone seagull picked at something near the pitcher's mound. In the distance, the quiet roar of the cars on the Don Valley Parkway could be heard. Corinne hoped he would say something good, the pause was so pregnant with meaning. But all he said was, "Do you think Albert Pujols is better than Miguel Cabrera?"

Corinne tried to get him back on track, but he would not say anything she liked. It was clear that he was better off – he was a normal little kid now, not some obese unsocialized compulsive-eating toddler – but she did not have a quote from him that said so.

"Jeremy," she said, "Let's play a game. I'm going to ask you a question, and I want you to give me an answer. I'm going to say, 'Two years later, what do you think of it all?', and you say, 'I like the way I am now.' Let's try it." She nodded to the cameraman. "Two years later, Jeremy, what do you think of everything that happened to you?" she asked.

Jeremy looked at her. "I like the way I am now?" he said, asking for approval.

"That was great!" said Corinne. "Let's just try it again. Only it's not a question, remember..."

They tried it four more times until they got it perfect. Then Corinne and the cameraman drove Jeremy to his father's house, where dinner and most of his family were waiting.

Michael's Pillow

In its tiny crib, the baby cried and cried. Its wail passed through the small hands of Michael, who had them pressed against his ears to keep out the wailing. When it got in anyway, he rolled over to look out the window. There was a tall dark oak tree that sparkled under the moon, God's beard rustling in the night. He asked God to stop the baby crying and watched the beard roll slightly from side to side, shaking his head No in the breeze. Michael wanted to get up and tell his mother to come, but Clyde was over. He always got whacked if he bothered her at night when Clyde was there, and Clyde laughed at him and gripped him in big hands and hairy knuckles. He wrapped the pillow around his head and waited.

In the next room, Michael's mother and Clyde lay naked on the bed. They did not hear the baby for a long time. Finally the music on the tape machine ran out with a clack, waking them back to the ordinary world.

"The baby," said its mother. She rolled away from Clyde and sat up on the bed, reaching for her underwear. Clyde grabbed her breasts from behind, pinching the nipples until she squealed. Hot milk trickled through his fingers.

"To hell with the baby, Bert," he said, and pulled her back. With an agile foot, Bert flicked the switch on the tape machine, and music from the radio filled the room.

One night Michael's mother had forgotten to pick him up at daycare, and he went home for dinner with the teacher, Mrs Redbock. Mrs Redbock's house had no elevator, she had a staircase and carpets and a hundred rooms. They had hot red meat at dinner and he tasted the blood mixed with

butter on his tongue. He sat on Mr Redbock's lap after
dinner and listened to him burp while they watched a
beautiful woman on television. Mrs Redbock tried to phone
his mother and he played with the other children. He liked a
red toy soldier and tried to hide it in his pocket, but it itched
and he took it out. Michael did not notice his mother was
there until she grabbed him by the arm and dragged him out
into the street. He was crying. Her breath smelled like old
bottles.

"Bitch," she said. "Who does she think she is?"

That was the day Bert found out she was three months
pregnant. She had had irregular periods before, ever since
she was a girl. Her friend Janet Blakey had the flu. Bert had
thought she was just regularly sick.

"Just get rid of it," Clyde said.

"What?" she said.

"You know. Get rid of it."

She had been thinking that since she felt the cold hands
of the doctor on her that morning, but she did not want to
agree with Clyde. "Why should I? Just because you say so?"

Michael was full of questions as the baby grew in her
belly.

"She's got a pillow in her stomach," said Clyde. "And
when they shake out the pillowcase, a baby comes out."

"Was I in there too?"

"You were in there too," said his mother.

"I didn't put you there," said Clyde.

"Maybe you didn't put this one there either," said
Michael's mother.

"To hell with all of you," said Clyde, and left. But
Michael was more interested in his mother's belly and the
baby inside it. That night, he pulled his pillow out of its case

and unzipped the side. It was filled with foam rubber that tasted of wood and pee.

When Clyde didn't come home for several days, Bert decided she did not need another child. She thought, one is trouble and expense enough. When Michael lay in bed that night, she told him she was not going to have a baby after all.

Michael did not understand at first. "Are you just going to keep it inside your stomach?" he asked.

She laughed and laughed until he laughed too, and she kept laughing even after he stopped and his ears glowed. "Keep it inside my stomach," she said. "No, I'm not going to keep in inside my stomach." And she explained that the doctor could take the baby out of her stomach and it would not be a baby, because it was too early.

But Michael was sleepy and could not understand. "What about the pillow?" he asked.

He's too young, she thought. "Don't you worry about that, honey," she said, and kissed him on the nose. "They just tie the pillowcase up," she pulled the blanket up under his chin, "and the baby inside has nowhere to go, so he just disappears." She turned out the light and left the room.

But when she went back to the doctor with the cold hands, he told her she was too late.

"No one here can do it for you. You should have made this decision a month ago." But he was a sympathetic man, and gave her the phone number of the clinic downtown. "They might be able to do it there," he said. "Our rules are more strict."

Later that week she still had not called the clinic when Clyde came home. He found the number stuck to the refrigerator with a magnet.

"What's this?" he asked.

"Nothing," she said, and threw the paper away.

In its crib, the baby cried and cried. Clyde and Michael's mother made their bed of love in the next room. Michael sang a song Mrs Redbock had taught them in daycare that week with the pillow wrapped around his head. When he ran out of verses, he removed the pillow. The baby stopped for a minute, but then began wailing louder than ever so that Michael's skin flinched and the tiny hairs on his neck stood up. He began to sing again, but the baby would not be quiet and he forgot the words. He got up from his bed and, holding the pillow, walked in four light steps to the crib. He climbed in. He slipped the case off and put it over the wailing baby's round head. The baby was quiet for a second, but then it started to wail again. The pillowcase turned wet over the baby's mouth. Michael pulled it over the baby's short waving arms, and pulled it down so that only the baby's feet were sticking out. The baby rolled and squirmed inside. It was still wailing. Michael pushed the baby's soft feet up and rolled the end around so that the feet were completely covered too. Then he went back to his own bed and lay with his head on the naked pillow, and waited for the baby to disappear.

IV. FAMILY STORIES

Terry and the Moon and Me

THE LAST TIME I saw my brother was through a window set inside a hospital door. Inside the glass were crossed wires that made the window a checkerboard and the room a prison, a child's game and sepulchre. I remember looking back over my Uncle's shoulder as he carried me away, the light from the room casting a glow into the dim corridor of the terminal wing, how his footsteps echoed and left no mark on the white and streaked tiles. In my dreams today I see the window turn into the moon and back into a window with the wire crosses in it, a fenced off hole of light punched in a wall. And I am on the wrong side, waiting until it is my turn to go into the room again, to learn what there is to learn there.

"Niagara Falls!" said Mom, and squeezed the washcloth against our shoulders. All the warm water went down our backs. Terry and I took baths together. Baths keep you clean, and being clean keeps you from being sick. Once when I was sick Dad brought me an airplane, so that was all right, but Mom made me stay in bed all day. If we just had a Dad, being sick would be fun, I thought, but Dad went to work all day and Mom just hung around the house. That's why we took baths.

When our bath was over, we had to put on our pyjamas and go to bed. But that was okay because Dad came in and read us a story. We liked it when Dad read us stories because he imitated all the voices. He could talk really high and really low. If he skipped a part, Terry and I would always yell that he was cheating. Then he would have to go back and read the part he skipped again.

He read the Bible. We liked the one about Samson and Delilah and the Philistines. Samson was as strong as Superman until Delilah cut all his hair off, and then he was weak until God made him strong enough to wreck the temple of the Philistines. Then he got buried under the temple. We asked Dad if Samson was fat because Dad was very fat. We wanted to be fat like Dad.

"Are you getting weak, Dad?" we asked. Dad's hair only covered the back part of his head.

"Am I getting weak?" he asked, and he looked very sad. We felt bad that we had asked, Terry and I, because he looked so sad.

Suddenly he yelled. "God has given me the strength to destroy you, oh evil Philistines!" and he laughed, and he grabbed us both up in his arms and swung us in the air while we screamed. It was great fun. He swung us back onto the bed and rolled the covers around us.

"And now, I will destroy your temple!" He picked up a pillow and hit us with it. We hit him with our pillows. We had a big fight and it was lots of fun, until Mom came in and told us to quit it. She looked very angry.

"But I'm Samson, and Samson has to destroy the evil Philistines!" Dad said. Mom looked angry, then she looked like she was about to throw up. But that was only because she was trying not to laugh, and then she did laugh, and she hit Dad with a pillow. Then Dad hit her with a pillow and she laughed and hit him with a pillow and we had a big pillow fight, the whole family. Mom and Terry and me were Philistines and Dad was Samson. When we were all tired out, Dad said we had to go to sleep, and if he heard one peep, he'd come in and hit us with Mom's jawbone. That meant Mom was a donkey, and she hit him and we laughed. Dad closed the blind and they left.

When it was winter, we would go outside in snowsuits and big boots. In winter your breath looks like smoke from a pipe and the inside of your nose feels like glass. Terry and I got to play outside in the back with Mom after lunch.

The ground was white and clean with snow. Terry and Mom and I ran around making footprints. "If you make footprints, you know where you've been," Mom said. "Footprints are tracks you can follow."

Terry and I had a contest rolling down the hill. We lay flat at the top and when Mom said "Go!" we rolled down. We had to do it three times because Mom could never tell who rolled faster, and then we got dizzy. Terry got snow in his coat the last time we rolled. It went down his back. Mom said we had to go in because it was too cold and we would catch triple pneumonia. We went inside and it was warm and it took a long time to get off all our clothes and Mom made us hot chocolate.

Dad was a doctor. That was why he was never home during the day. A doctor kills germs that make you sick. Dad was looking after other people all day.

He showed us in the front of the Bible where our names were written and our birthdays and christenings. A christening is where your name comes from. There was also marriages where he and Mom were written, and places for military service and deaths. Those places were blank.

Mom always did housework in the morning, so Terry and I played together by ourselves a lot. Terry was younger than me, and he didn't know very much sometimes. He asked questions all the time, but I could never answer them. I thought he might be stupid, because I never understood where he got the questions from.

Terry and I had twin beds against the wall opposite the window of our room. One night after our story Dad forgot to close the shade. The moon was shining half full above the poplar tree in the park.

"Why do you think the moon shines like that?" he said.

"I don't know. Maybe it's like a light bulb." A little grey cloud crossed in front of the moon and disappeared.

"You know what I think? I think someone punched a hole in the side of the night. That's why the moon is bright. Because it's daytime coming in through a hole."

I knew it was wrong, but I didn't know what to say. Then I knew. I said, "Oh yeah? Well where is the daytime at night?"

Terry sat up. "It's behind the night. The night goes in front of the day. It's like the blind on the window. And the moon is like a hole."

The next day we asked Mom. She said Terry was wrong. I said the earth was in the middle and the sky was like the inside of a ball going around the earth. Half the ball was light and half the ball was dark. When the light half was up, it was daytime, and when the dark half was up, it was night.

Mom said that still didn't explain what the moon was. She drew a picture of a bunch of circles. The one in the middle was the sun, and the earth and moon were beside it. The earth was a ball that spun around once a day, and when it spun away from the sun, then it was night. The moon spun around the earth and shone because the sun made it light up. That part sounded like what Terry thought.

When we went to bed that night, Terry said, "I don't think Mom is very smart." I asked him why. He said, "If

the earth spins, how come we don't feel it spin? And if the
sun lights up the moon, why can't we see the moon better in
the daytime?" So we decided that the moon was a hole in
the side of the night that let day in. But we decided not to
tell Mom about it, in case she felt bad.

Terry and I were five years old at the time. Sometimes I
was older but sometimes I wasn't. That winter we had
check-ups with a doctor – not Dad, since he was a special
kind of doctor. Terry's bloodtest showed leukemia. Mom
explained to me that Terry was very sick and he got all the
attention and I wished I had leukemia too so I could get
another airplane. Terry didn't seem any different, except he
had to go to the doctor every week and take a lot of
medicine. At first I wanted to take medicine too, but when I
saw how it tasted and how many needles he got I didn't want
it anymore.

We were in the hospital. Terry and I sat on the bed and
Dad read to us about Beowulf and the dragon. Then Dad
asked if we wanted a tuna-fish sandwich. I said okay. Terry
said he wasn't very hungry and could he have just a one-a-
fish sandwich. Dad liked that a lot, and we all had one-a-fish
sandwiches.

Terry had to stay in the hospital longer and longer that
winter. There was nothing to do during the day. Dad
bought me a Lego set. Lego was bricks you could use to
build things with. The bricks were red and blue and yellow
and black. Dad and I built a building and a man and a plane.
It was dark out, and the moon was a small white circle in the
middle of our window. A plane flew by under the moon.
You can tell planes because they look like different coloured
stars that move and blink.

"Can planes fly through the moon, Dad?"

"What's that?"

"Planes. Can they fly through the moon? To get to the daytime on the other side." He asked what I meant. "Terry says the moon is a hole in the side of the night, and that daytime comes through it, even at night. Like a hole in the blind."

"Oh." He looked out the window. The sky was navy blue, the same colour the sailor suits Terry and I wore when we had to go visiting. It was cold and hard, and the moon looked cold and liquid, like milk.

"We could fly through the moon in a plane and it would always be day and you and me and Mom and Terry could all be together, and it could be soft grass and we could read stories and have pillow fights."

Dad smiled. Then he looked sad. "I don't think planes can fly to the moon anymore Joseph," he said. Then he talked for a long time about Adam and Eve and the garden on the other side of the moon, and how a snake tricked them so that God put them on our side of the moon, and how we could never go back there until we died. He looked very sad, and I was sad too. Then Mom came in and we had to go to the hospital again.

The hospital was very big and had white tile floors with streaks in them. We had to walk down a lot of hallways to get to Terry. The beds in the hospital aren't like the beds at home. They have levers and things in the end, and you can make them higher or lower or sit up. And they have bars so you won't fall out. Terry's bed was in the sitting up position, and he was looking out the window when we came in. When he looked at us, I noticed that he was going bald and getting fat. He looked like he was holding his breath, but he wasn't. I was scared.

"Hi Terry!" Mom said. She gave him a big hug and he smiled, and then I wasn't scared anymore. I jumped up on the bed and sat beside him.

Terry had a table that reached across his bed. It had blocks on it, and we started to pile them up. Dad started to help us, and Mom watched and drank coffee. We built a temple and then Terry got to be Samson and knock it over. Then I got to be Samson, and then we told Dad to be Samson too, but he looked sad.

He said, "Raze my temple, and in three days I shall rebuild it." We looked at him. We didn't know what he meant, but we were too scared to ask him. He took the temple apart slowly, without knocking it at all, as if it were made of glass. Then Terry said, "Boom!" and knocked it all over. First we laughed, but Dad still looked sad, and we were scared.

A nurse came in. She was thin and white, like an angel. "Hello Terry," she said. "Is your family visiting you?"

He said, "Yup."

"And I bet this is your brother," she said and leaned up close to me. She smelled good.

"Yup."

"Well, I'm Helen, Terry's nurse. Hello Mr Lucowitz. Mrs Lucowitz. Terry's been a wonderful patient."

"He's a doctor," Terry said.

"Yeah." Dad and the nurse went out into the hall and talked quietly. Then Mom went out into the hall too. Terry and I sat on the bed.

"Is it fun being here?" I said.

"It's okay. They don't let me go outside. It's boring."

"Oh." It felt funny sitting on Terry's bed because it wasn't his real bed. I got under the covers with him.

"Now we can have leukemia together," I said.

"Now we can both be fat!"

"Like Dad!"

"Like Samson!"

"Boom!" We knocked all the blocks off the bed onto the floor, and they bounced and made echoing noises. Then we were scared, but Mom and Dad were out in the hall and Dad only looked in and then they went back to talking. We sat without saying anything for a little while.

Then Terry said, "You can't see the moon from here."

I looked out the window. It was all cloudy. "But you can see the street lights. It doesn't matter even if it's cloudy. And there's more of them."

"They're just light bulbs."

I was getting mad. "But they're just as good as the moon. There's more of them, and it can be cloudy, and you can always see them." I was almost crying.

"It's not the same."

I was crying, so I hit him, and then he hit me and I hit him again, and then Dad was there and picked me up and Mom sat with Terry, and he was crying too.

"Joseph, don't you know your brother is sick?" Mom was whispering at me because you can't yell in a hospital, but I was crying and Dad carried me away, and he kept patting my head and saying, "There there, don't cry Joseph," and soon I stopped until he asked me what was wrong and then I started again and he said it again and I stopped again and this time he didn't ask me. He rocked me in his arms slowly so that I felt warm and safe. I said, "I don't want Terry to have leukemia anymore," and we went back to his room.

After a while we had to say good-bye to Terry and go home. It was late. On the ride home it was foggy and the narrow rows of street lights spread open to let our car through and closed up again as we passed. The apartment buildings on the hill were building blocks with stars in them.

When we got home Mom made Dad and I hot chocolate. We made a hospital out of Lego, but it was no good. Dad and I went upstairs to bed, and he sat down on Terry's bed to read. Mom came in and sat on the bed with Dad. We sat there for a long time, and I was scared. Mom and Dad were sitting close together, the way they did when Mom would giggle, but they looked sad.

"Joseph," Dad said. He stopped. Then he said, "Terry isn't coming home anymore."

"Oh." I said. "Can we still go see him in the hospital?"

Dad stopped. He and Mom looked at each other. Then he said that we could go to the hospital tomorrow to see Terry.

I had two dreams that night. I was sitting in a hospital bed in an empty white room. There was no door and no windows, just white ceiling, floor, and walls. Then there were footprints on the floor, and I thought it was snow. I tried to look around for the sky, or to dig beneath the snow, but I couldn't. Everything was white, even the sky, and then I couldn't tell if I was inside or outside, and I had to look at the footprints or else my head would ache from looking at the white everywhere. I followed the footprints for a long time. But when I looked behind me, they were all gone, and there was only white. Then I knew that my own tracks were erasing the tracks I had followed, and I left nothing but white behind. There was nothing for me to do but keep following the trail in front of me to find out who made it and where he had gone. But the trail stopped and I was left alone in a great field of nothing but white. I tried to make a mark on the ground but I couldn't. I was about to cry, but then I saw a black spot far in the distance, small as an eyeball, and I went toward it. It was my own hospital bed, but when I climbed on, I made it disappear too, and I disappeared in it, and there was nothing left anywhere but white.

Later I had another dream. I was in an airplane at night and I flew to the moon. I was going to fly through it to find the daytime on the other side, but a wall went up in front of it in blue, red, yellow, and black bricks. The wall turned into a building that covered me and crushed me down until the airplane got smaller and smaller, so small that it could fit in a hospital room like a bed. Then the nurse came in and said, "Do you have leukemia like your brother?" And then I shouted no and told her Dad was a doctor and he would kill her, but he never came and she shaved my hair and turned into a snake. She opened her mouth wide to eat me, so wide that I could see Terry in her stomach, and I began to scream.

Then Dad came in and I was awake. "It was a dream."

"How come you don't cure Terry?" He said what, and I asked it again. "Why don't you kill the leukemia germs?"

Dad looked very sad. I had never seen him look so sad, and he said, "There are some germs that you can't kill." He talked for a long time about specialists and germs and leukemia. The germs were eating up Terry's insides, and I knew that a germ was a snake inside you, the same snake that put us all on the wrong side of the moon. And then I knew that the snake was something that even Dad couldn't kill, because it was older than him, older than anything, a snake from a long time ago. And I knew that Dad wasn't really Samson, and there was nothing he could do.

I was crying, and Dad picked me up and carried me to the living room while I hugged his shoulder. We sat together in the rocking chair and looked out the window. The fog had lifted. On the ground, the snow was less, and dark grass and earth were peeking out into the night. Dad rocked slowly back and forth and hummed a song he used to sing to Terry and I, and I put my arms around his neck and fell asleep.

We saw Terry in the hospital. One day when we went, they had moved him to a different place and we had to walk all around. I was tired, so Dad carried me in his arms. We passed rooms with open doors and people lying in beds. In one room there was a man with no legs. In another was a man who was all bandages. In one was a man who had a normal head but his body was small, smaller than a pot. We came to a room with the door closed. Dad put me down on a chair in the hall and told me to wait quietly. He and Mom went and talked to a doctor.

Dad came and put a white mask over my face. He had one on too. He said it would be just like Hallowe'en, but it wasn't much fun and your breath felt hot inside the mask. Then we went into the room to see Terry.

Terry was lying in bed. His face was white, and he was very fat and bald. He was sweating. He looked tired, because he didn't move when we came in.

"Hi," he said. His voice was scratchy. Mom sat on the bed beside him and held his hand. Her eyes were big, and I could tell she was crying but trying not to show. Dad and I sat on the bed across from Mom, on the other side of Terry.

"How come you don't have any toys?" I said. Dad said Terry was too tired to play with toys. Terry said his arms and legs hurt. Then we sat still and I tried hard not to make any noise.

The doctor came in. Uncle Tom came in. We were all wearing white masks over our noses and mouths. After a while Dad picked me up and told me to say good-bye to Terry, but Terry was sleeping. Dad held me in one arm and pressed Terry's hand. He woke up, and Dad said, "Say good-bye to your brother, Joseph."

Terry said good-bye. Uncle Tom carried me out of the room. They closed the door behind us. There was a window in the door, and we turned around to look. I waved good-bye to Terry through the glass, but he didn't see it. Then Mom and Dad and the doctor and the nurse crowded around the bed and we left. Uncle Tom's walking sounded hollow in the empty hall. I watched the room fade away as he carried me.

Later Mom and Dad told me that Terry had died that day and that he wouldn't be coming home anymore but that he was in heaven with God and that we would all be with him some day and that nothing could hurt him anymore. And I remember thinking then that that was pretty good, and that I would be a good boy.

Beautiful Kai

This story takes place in Nigeria, the home of the man from whom I heard it.

THERE WAS A WOMAN named Kai who was so lovely that everyone called her Beautiful Kai. She had a baby son.

One night, Beautiful Kai's aunt, the wise woman in the village, saw a dead spot in the fire. She stirred the coals, but the dead spot reappeared. She stirred the coals again, but again the dead spot appeared. Three times she stirred the coals, and three times the dead spot appeared. After that she poured water on the fire and wrapped herself in a blanket to wait for what would happen.

The next day, Beautiful Kai left the baby sleeping while she went to the well. When she returned, her hut was on fire and the baby shrieking inside. She ran into the hut to save the baby, forgetting even to throw the water on the flames. The thatched roof collapsed on them, but she shielded the child with her body and escaped through a flaming wall. She tore her burning clothes off and rolled naked on the dusty ground to put out the fire that covered her.

She could not move for three months. A wet nurse and foster mother were found for the baby boy. The village women cared for her and smeared her burns with an ointment made from cinders and animal fat. Her husband wept when he saw her. He said he needed a woman, not an ash-heap, and left for another village. Beautiful Kai told the other women: "I did not bear a son to leave him to the fire." At night the flames visited her in her dreams and she clawed herself with burnt fingers.

When she was able to walk again, her face and body were covered over with bulging pink scars. She had neither hair nor eyebrows nor eyelashes, and she learned to do everything at night to avoid being burned by the sun.

Her sister told her about their aunt and the dead spot in the fire. "She saved you. She put the fire out and spent the night wrapped in blankets so that you and your boy would live."

Another woman said, "The fire wanted to sell your boy to Death. You got there before Death, and shielded the boy from him. But the fire had his revenge on you."

Beautiful Kai disagreed with both. She said, "My boy was born for something. God has a plan for him, a plan that is stronger than fire."

Wars and revolutions came, and many of the men were forced to leave and become soldiers. The fighting came to their village, and with no men the women had to move away, heading first south, then east, then south, always along the river. One night soldiers came and took the other women for themselves, even the old ones, but they left Beautiful Kai because with her scars she was too ugly. Beautiful Kai continued along the river.

The wars ended and Beautiful Kai and her boy settled in the south. She stopped dreaming of fire and the sun no longer hurt her, and she found a job as a labourer on a cacao plantation. Her son grew and was called Kanuri, because they were the only people from that tribe in the area.

*

Kanuri was ashamed. He was about to graduate from school and his mother wanted to come. He did not want her to come. He did not want the boys and girls in his class to see how ugly she was. He did not want Sister Oya to see her. He did not want the other priests and nuns to see her. He did not want the girl he intended to marry to see her. But she wanted to come.

It was because she was impressed, he realized now. He had spoken too much about it. Pride was his downfall, just as Sister Oya had taught. He had boasted about his brilliance, about his wisdom. He had told her how the teachers praised him. He had told her about the planned graduation ceremony, how each of the students would line up and receive a diploma from the Bishop, how a famous white plantation owner would give a speech. The students would all wear gowns like the Englishmen wore at Oxford University, and there would be a band.

He saw now that he had made the ceremony sound too grand. "And what day is this graduation, so that I may tell Mr Whipley that I will not work that day?" his mother asked.

Kanuri was about to tell her, then stopped. It was then he realized that he would be undone if his mother came to the graduation. "I do not know what day it is," he lied. "But I will find out."

Years before, when they had first settled in the south, Kanuri worked on the plantation with his mother. But Beautiful Kai had let Kanuri know that it was not his fate to spend all his days in the fields. "I have read your destiny in the eyes of the fire," she told him. "You were not made for this. You will walk with the great." As if in fulfillment of her prophecy, a white priest appeared at the plantation one day, and Kanuri was chosen to start at the Mission School.

He felt his mother's confidence that God had created him for some great thing, though what it would be he did not yet know. Sometimes he thought of asking her what great thing awaited him, but he never did – at first because it was too frightening; later because what his mother thought seemed irrelevant.

School was a long distance from the plantation. Kanuri walked three miles to a crossroads every morning, then got on a bus full of children.

Kanuri loved school. A clean dusky brown nun in a smock and habit taught them about Jesus Christ and the prophet Moses, about Great Britain where the Queen and Winston Churchill and the Beatles all lived, about America where there are lights and money and everyone drives his own car and drinks Coca-Cola. Her name was Sister Oya. She had a British accent and smelled of flowers and soap. Kanuri loved her.

He learned to look at maps and see the rivers and the seas and the land. He learned to read. Sometimes Kanuri brought his books home and read them to his mother in their hut. He read stories from the Bible, from Grimm's Fairy Tales, and from A Boy's History of the British Empire. He showed his mother the maps in his atlas, but she was unable to understand them. Kanuri would point to a spot just west of the town and say, "We live here." Then his mother would point to a neighbouring country, Benin or the Cameroon or Niger and say, "So Mr Whipley lives here." Mr Whipley owned the plantation and lived in a great house on the hill.

As Kanuri grew older, he began to work at the plantation house when school was out. He checked columns of numbers against the items unloaded off a truck for one of

Mr Whipley's men, Mr MacKenzie. At first Mr MacKenzie checked his numbers after he did them. But as time passed, he checked them less and less. "You're all right, boyo," he said, and patted Kanuri's head with a thick hard hand. Kanuri was very proud of his work for Mr MacKenzie, and little by little he was able to do more and more.

One day he overheard Mr MacKenzie and another man talking out on the porch of the great plantation house. They were talking about the workers on the plantation, and they mentioned his mother.

"Beautiful Kai?" said an Englishman's voice.

"The scarred one," said Mr MacKenzie.

"The ugly one?"

"Yes."

"It's interesting that they call her 'Beautiful Kai', since that's a kind of irony these Africans don't usually indulge."

Kanuri would read the dictionaries and encyclopaediae at school to learn what irony was, but it was years before he was sure of the Englishman's meaning. It was after he overheard this conversation, however, that he became ashamed of his mother.

At school, Kanuri began to notice how beautiful the people were. All the children had smooth dark skin and deep brown eyes. Their faces were symmetrical in shape and simple. He imagined how easy drawing their faces would be. The white nuns and priests who taught them had more lines and blue and green eyes, their skin was pale, their hair thin and floppy, but their faces too were simple and symmetrical, as if God had built only half a face and filled the other half in with a mirror. Kanuri knew that he himself was beautiful, his face too was half a face with a perfect image of itself on the other side. He looked at himself in the mirror in school and in the pools and ponds on his way home to see his half face multiplied.

At home, Kanuri looked at his mother. Her face was hideous and misshapen. There were great irregular pink and wrinkled ridges all up and down, above her eyes, across her nose, cutting up her cheeks. Her eyes were hidden beneath one of these ridges and peered out like tiny black fish. One of her ears was nothing but a small hole on the side of her head. There was a deep scarred fold below her chin that she had to wash every morning and night or else it began to smell like a man's navel. There was none of the beautiful symmetry of the faces at school. It was as if God had thrown a wet ball of mud on top of his mother's scarred body and breathed life into it.

Kanuri worked hard at the plantation house and at school. He hoped to become a priest and go to England some day, or even to America, where he might buy his own car and drive to Texas. Now he pretended to be tired and made excuses to be away from home so that he would not have to see his mother, the ugly Beautiful Kai. He was glad he lived far away from the school. He had fallen in love with a girl there, and he did not want her to see his mother. In his dreams, he married the girl and had a baby, but when the child came from the womb she had the hideous face of his mother...

As graduation came nearer, he started avoiding home more than ever, sleeping at the huts of friends or in Mr Whipley's stables and garage or even out in the open. All his nightmares now ended with the image of his mother's grotesque face coming between him and everything desirable in life. He was sure he would never be married if anyone saw his mother.

He hoped that Beautiful Kai would forget about the graduation ceremony. He hoped that he might sneak off to it and come back to apologize to her that it was all over. But whenever she saw him, she asked him when it would be. He continued to pretend that he did not know, but would find out soon. He knew it was a sin not to honour your mother, but he began to pray to God that she would not attend the ceremony. He began to hate her, who would ruin his life just to satisfy her curiosity and pride.

One day he was dawdling back home after school when his mother called him. "Kanuri, Kanuri."

He went to her.

"You should not be doing what you are doing," she told him.

He was amazed that she had found him out. Her face was more hideous than ever. Her little black eyes peered out at him from beneath her flaming pink brow. He said nothing, hating her with a silent hatred. He would not allow her to ruin his graduation.

"You are dishonouring both yourself and the woman," she said. "A woman who has already known a man will not receive a large dowry. It is not for this that you were born."

For a moment Kanuri was stunned. He realized: his mother was stupider than he had thought. "I dishonour no one," he told her. And he grew so angry he told her everything: that she was ugly, that no one would marry him if they knew what his daughters would look like, that no one would speak to him again at the graduation if they knew his mother was a hideous northerner with a face like a ball of wet mud whom people called Beautiful Kai only in mockery. He poured all the bitterness of his heart over her. When that was spent, he began to cry, and he begged her not to come to his graduation.

His mother was silent through it all. She stood silently until he had stopped for a more than a minute. He stared at her, then put his head down. He felt as though he were about to be executed. Then Beautiful Kai said, "I will not come to your graduation if you ask me again not to come."

Joy filled Kanuri.

"But before you ask again, you must listen. And I will tell you how I lost my beauty and received my scars."

In the Pale Light that Each Upon the Other Throws

THEY FOUND MY GREAT GRANDMOTHER Anne sitting with her back against Willie McCover's gravestone. She was dressed in a nightgown and rubber boots and wore a kerchief around her head. In one hand, she held the spade. She had made a hole about one foot deep and two feet wide, and sat down to rest. The hole was half filled with rainwater, and she was soaked.

It was not the first time she had snuck off to Willie McCover's grave. She had done it many times before, and one of the children was always assigned the task of looking after her. She would get up on a warm summer night and say, "I think I'll go for a little walk," or she would be seen disappearing through the apple orchard under the moonlight, or they would hear a creak on the stairs or the sound of a chair bumped in the darkness or the door gently shutting, and that would be my great grandmother stealing away to her Willie McCover beneath the great oak tree in the cemetery. Sometimes she would have pie or cookies with her, or, if the snow or moon were bright, a book. She always pretended these things were snacks for her walk or a book for when she would stop and sit down, but they would find the pie plate on the grave the next day, or catch her sitting under the moonlight reading to Willie.

"What was she like when they caught her?" we little ones would ask.

Nonchalant, they told us. A son or daughter would come, or, in the old days, Father Farrell, whose window looked out across the cemetery, and he would say, "Mrs LeRoy?" and she would look up and say, "Oh, hello, is that you?" and comment that the weather was fine, or the rain was good for the farmers, or that she loved to walk in the snow, and then she would walk home and that would be that. But the next night, she would often as not be back.

In the last two years of her life things got worse. Where before she had always taken meticulous care of her appearance and wore her Sunday hat and gloves to the cemetery, she began to neglect herself and would be found wearing a nightgown and gardening boots with her Sunday hat, or winter boots in the middle of summer, or her husband's old overcoat and high-heeled shoes. She began to do more than speak to Willie McCover, and she would be found lying across his grave, or she would take a garden hoe or the spade with her and begin to dig at it. One night she got out in the middle of a blizzard, and if she hadn't gotten turned around in the snow and ended up back at the house knocking things over on the porch, that might have been the end of her.

"Why didn't you watch her more carefully to make sure she didn't get out?" we asked, because we were young. We believed then that you could prevent people from doing things that were bad for them.

That's the way it was, they always said. One day when we asked, our grandfather told us that you can't keep Rapunzel locked in the tower forever, you have to let her out to see the prince. You can't spend your whole life watching someone else to make sure they don't leave you, he said. So one rainy night when no one was watching, my great grandmother left in a thunderstorm with her spade and her rubber boots, her nightgown and her kerchief, to free Willie McCover from his grave and be with him once more. She had been dead for two hours, the doctor said, before he got there. She was eighty-seven years old.

That was where the story ended. It began more than seventy years earlier: my great grandmother, then Anne Johnston, at the age of seventeen. She was wearing a new dress, with white lace, blue sash, puffed sleeves, and long skirt, her orange hair glowing in the late afternoon sun, her arm raised to throw a stick to the dog, her laughter. Her younger sister Nancy was screaming, and her mother was calling her to come in and not to spoil the new dress. Her feet were bare and muddy. "I remember it all as if it were an hour ago," my great grandfather would say. "The stick, the raised arm, the orange hair, the white and blue, the bare muddy feet." He would describe the scene at Christmas and Easter dinner every year, and many times in between.

This was my great grandfather's particular genius: that he was able to take a single moment and hold it in his memory forever, a single instant acquiring for him a characterizing force and presence that time could not darken. His name was Jack LeRoy.

Jack remembered that instant of careless beauty the way he did not remember, for instance, the time Anne was thirteen years old and he met her, panting and breathless and dirty, in front of the rectory, when she said hello and then ran off, and how five minutes later he met her father the judge on the same road looking for her with a leather belt in his hand. Nor did he remember so well the time he saw her on a warm spring night, with Willie McCover holding her hand on the path to the graveyard behind the old church, and that Willie tried to leave the path when he saw Jack in the distance but Anne pulled him back and the two walked straight up to him and past him, Anne swinging Willie's hand in hers, and Anne said in her light Scots burr, "Good evening to you, Mr Jack LeRoy, and to where are you off tonight?" as if challenging him to ask to where she and Willie McCover were off. But Jack was not the type to ask, and he said good evening and continued on his road.

We heard those last stories about Anne only once, at Easter in the late 1960s, when the adults were talking about all the trouble the Americans were having with their young people. My great grandfather himself seemed surprised as he recalled those episodes, intimations of Anne's wildness, as if he had never had any reason to think of them before. And even while in memory he heard Anne giggling and Willie whispering on the road behind him, what he saw instead was the perfect picture of Anne in her white dress with the blue sash, her orange hair and the sunshine of her mother's front yard. He put the other recollections down quickly, as if he had picked up a letter addressed to someone he did not know, and picked up instead the Anne he loved to remember, telling us yet again about their dog, the stick, the muddy feet. It was because of that vision that Jack happened to fall in love with Anne on a warm spring day in 1914, and because of the invincible focus of his memory that he would love her for the rest of her life and even unto death.

On the evening that he fell in love with her, Anne Johnston saw him walking past and interrupted her game with the dog to call him over to say hello. She told him that her mother had just finished the dress. "Do you like it, now?" she said, and spun in a little turn for him.

Jack stood and nodded. He stared at Anne's face. She was smiling and her eyes were bright green. Jack, then a year behind her at school, suddenly became nervous. It occurred to him that he should ask her to the tea dance. She wants me to, he thought. As he realized this, he seemed to see in her eyes a change, as if they were no longer just looking, but now encouraging him to speak. It was an interesting change, he always said, and later he often attributed it to his own hopefulness and not any real change on Anne's part. He decided he must ask her, and thought about what he would say. He was already showing signs of the patience that would characterize him later in life.

He missed the moment. "Is tha Jack LeRoy, noo?" said Anne's mother, trundling down the hill from the house. She spoke in a thick Scots accent. "Wha din yu invite hem in, Annie?" She turned to Jack. "Would yu lahk a glass of milk, Jack? Wha din yu ask yur parents to stop by an vizet us some time, noo?"

Nancy, who had been playing with the dog, said, "Jack is trying to get up the courage to ask Anne to the tea dance." It was about the time that Nancy spoke that he began to feel his asthma coming on.

Mrs Johnston looked at Nancy, then at Anne, then at Jack, who felt his throat burning. She said, "Will, for heaven's sake, dinna let me stop yu, boy." But the attack came, and Jack could not speak, and Mrs Johnston sent Nancy to the house to bring water.

The next day, Jack learned that Anne was going to the dance with Willie McCover, who was two years older than Jack and had dropped out of school three years before.

Willie McCover's father had once played professional hockey in Toronto and before that won a medal killing Indians in Texas, but he was also a shiftless man who drank too much and beat his son. One day, the story went, he had told his son that he would be better off without him, a formulation which left who would be better off without whom unclear. Whichever way he meant it, he hopped a westbound freight and never came back. Red Underhill, the postman, said he had a letter with an Arkansas postmark for Willie once, but nothing before or since.

Willie was a wild boy. No one blamed him for it, since his father's desertion was well-known. Willie had been taken into the rectory by Father Farrell, then went to live with the Conovers when it was thought that the presence of both a father and mother might do him good. He beat the Conover son, Seamus, black and blue over the rights to a pair of skates, and threw a frying pan of hot grease at Mrs Conover in her own kitchen. After that he dropped out of school and lived in a boarding house by the railroad, where he learned to drink and swear and spit tobacco juice. He was famous among the boys in town because he had a tremendous slapshot and he had once hopped a freight train to follow his father and was brought back by a mountie.

That spring, despite the objections of her mother and father, Anne took Willie to the tea dance, and the two were inseparable all summer. Jack, who was working for Mr Quill at the bank, saw them downtown in the afternoon drinking lemonades and walking arm in arm. Willie McCover wore an old suit that was too small for him. Anne walked with her head high, wore white gloves and carried a purse. She greeted everyone she knew – which was nearly everyone in town – with a formal 'Good day to you, Mrs _____, I hope you are feeling well,' as if she were a debutante in a novel. She introduced Willie McCover to everyone – 'Have you met Mr McCover?' – and stared at them through fierce green eyes, daring anyone to be rude to her and her beau. Willie McCover endured these walks through town in a distant, almost embarrassed silence. Some of the ladies in town took to crossing the street to avoid meeting Anne and Willie, and

Anne would call out to them from across the street – 'Good day to you, Mrs _____!' The ladies talked to Mrs Johnston about the terrible goings on with her daughter, but nothing changed. When Mrs Johnston talked to Anne, she refused to listen. When Anne's father stopped giving her any allowance, she stole it from his wallet. When she was forbidden to go outside and locked indoors, she climbed out the window into the old willow tree, and was seen that very afternoon on King St with Willie McCover on one arm and white gloves on her hands, wishing a good day to everyone she met and introducing them to Mr McCover.

If that had been the end of it, there might have been no harm. But that was not the end of it. The news came and spread quickly. Judge Johnston's daughter, the spoiled one, and Willie McCover, the wild boy whose father was the war hero, poor man, those two beneath the oak tree in the graveyard – the tree of knowledge of good and evil, they called it, the great black-hearted oak. Judge Johnston had found them out, he had had indigestion from too much steak and mushrooms – Judge Johnston was partial to steak and mushrooms, it was well-known – and he heard the dog barking and whining, and looked out and saw his eldest daughter disappearing down the hill in the moonlight in the direction of the canal. He dressed and took his shotgun and the dog and went off in Anne's direction, the dog snuffling and excited.

What happened next depended upon whom you believed, and the story began to grow as soon as it began. The judge shouting, 'You'll never disgrace my house again,' and firing twice, Anne leaping in front of the bullets and crying, 'Father, Willie is my one true love,' and, in early versions, shot by her own father in the graveyard, given the Last Rites by Father Farrell (who, according to his enemies, had been awakened by the noise from a drunken stupor and wore only his nightshirt and overcoat), and Anne dying in the arms of both her father and Willie McCover, the two at last reconciled by her death.   There was an equally popular version, circulating among a different crowd, that Willie McCover thought the white-haired judge was a ghost and he stood up and turned tail naked as a jaybird, and the first he realized it wasn't a spook from the grave was when he felt the judge's buckshot on his backside, and he fell down and got up again and over that graveyard wall and never stopped running until he reached Halifax.

Jack heard a thousand variations on the story.   "I've always said that Anne Johnston was no good.   She is vain and headstrong and her father was too liberal with her.   It's no surprise to me," said Mrs Oliphant, one of the bank tellers and a very moral woman.   The romantic version of the story – where Anne dies in the arms of her father and Willie McCover – collapsed when Anne was seen going to confession with the Johnston family before Saturday evening vespers.   She was puffy-eyed and not nearly so proud as she had been on her downtown promenades with Willie McCover, and she looked down at the ground and slightly to the left, keeping close to her parents and barely saying hello. Since she had not died heroically for love, more and more people – particularly women – were inclined to agree with Mrs Oliphant: she was spoiled and good for nothing, already a ruined woman at the age of seventeen.   The men were more indulgent, but that was only because – as Mrs Oliphant told her customers – "men were no good at all, at all, and if there were not good women to keep them in line they would trade places with Willie McCover in a second.   And they would amount to as much as Willie McCover too.   Which is nothing at all, at all." Many people were forced to agree that she was absolutely right.

The gossip about Anne Johnston and Willie McCover might have kept on, but less than one week later the Germans marched into Belgium. Britain declared war and Canada was at war too, and there was more to talk about than the indiscretions of spoiled youth. In the early excitement, the feeling was that the confining days of the small colonial world were over, that it was time for largesse, for heroism, for the passage from national child to adult through the ordeals of water and fire. The boys from the school — whose peace-time prospects were dull at best — made their way to Peterborough and even Toronto to sign up. They had grown to young manhood in a cold poor land less than fifty years old, a land of no history except as an adjunct of the great Empire. They were eager to get out and have their war: to leave the dusty small town and land on the shores of Europe with guns in their hands, to save a grateful people and punish an evil one. When King Albert went into exile and the Germans reached France, it was all the more clear that the colonials were needed, that the Canadian boys would show Europe how it was done, and der Kaiser's nose would be bloodied and his henchmen scurrying back to Berlin in defeat.

Because of his asthma, Jack LeRoy could not go to the war. By the summer of 1915, he was the only man in town under the age of twenty-three, and by 1916 the only man under the age of thirty. He quickly became head teller at the bank as senior positions held by older men were vacated. He became an important man in town as well, simply because there were always things that needed to be done that were easiest for a young man. He repaired the Taubensees' roof, he built a new fence around Mrs Bakerfeld's pasture, he dug up the old septic tank in the Johnston's yard and planted a new one. He dug holes for privies and fixed anything that needed fixing. His father contracted pneumonia one winter night and died, and Mr Quill gave him a small raise. His mother went to live with his married sister in Peterborough and stayed to work in the new recruiting office.

Jack took to spending time with Fr Farrell, the old priest. Every Saturday they would sit by his fireplace drinking beer (although the province of Ontario passed prohibition that year, Fr Farrell had taken the precaution of lining his cellar walls with bottles of Sudbury's Silver Foam) and playing backgammon for three cents a game. After a few beers, Fr Farrell would begin to talk. His favourite topics were humility and love, Christianity and romanticism.

"The romantic," he would say, "thinks of himself at the centre of the story. The world exists only for him to do his heroic deeds. The Christian, on the other hand, knows that he is not the centre, knows that he is as far from the centre as can be. The Christian understands that he lives at the margin of life. That is why Christianity is stronger than romanticism, because inevitable suffering and mediocrity destroy the romantic's image of himself and destroy his will, but they bring the Christian nearer to the centre. And here is another thing, Jack," he would say, "the romantic can never understand the Christian, but the Christian can see everyone."

Jack loved these afternoons. The pride he felt in discussing philosophy with the priest – even if Fr Farrell did most of the talking – was deepened by the thrill of their subversive activities: smoking, drinking beer and gambling. The fact that he had not been man enough to go to war (as he thought in his darkest times) had been a blow, and the masculine friendship of the priest was important to him. It did not occur to him at the time that Fr Farrell was a weak man and that his speeches were excuses for his own lack of will. In Fr Farrell's philosophizing, Jack heard only an allegory of Anne Johnston, the self-centred romantic heroine, and himself, her one true and Christian lover who waited for her on the margins of the world.

Because Jack was still waiting for Anne Johnston. He had met her several times since Willie McCover ran away: he saw her in the bank, running errands for her father, at the church they both attended, even at the Johnston home where he visited and occasionally did odd jobs. On those occasions, it sometimes seemed to him that she had lost something: that the fullness of her personality, once so proud and strong, had turned instead to a lack, a brittle defiance, like an actress who had once been beautiful but now was only painted. Then he would remember her as he had seen her that spring day before the war, before Willie McCover, before the tea dance, and he would see the old Anne Johnston in her young girl's beauty again. This vision of the perfect Anne would fill his sight, and he would rededicate his life to hers, telling himself that his patience was stronger than her pride, that he had only to wait long enough for her to love him, because the love of Christ was stronger than the posturing of the romantics.

On their afternoons together, Fr Farrell's conversation would always run off in one of two directions, each meaning it was time for Jack to go. He would begin to denounce the war and Canada's involvement in it ("I was in Ireland in 1904, Jack, and let me tell you, the Kaiser is the judgment of God against the sins of the Empire"), or he would begin again to hint that Jack ought to join the priesthood ("Only a romantic starts a war, Jack. And the priest is his true enemy. This war is British romanticism against German romanticism. What is needed is not more romantics with guns, but Christianity, and Jack, ...”). Jack would sometimes try to move Fr Farrell off the war and around to the people in town and Anne Johnston, but once he began on politics the priest never stopped. He cursed Borden, said there was no politician a Catholic could rightly vote for in this province, and then returned again to the war or the British in Ireland. Jack would make an excuse and leave the rectory, and as he walked home he was always mildly pleased with himself that he never confided in Fr Farrell about Anne, nor in anyone else, but kept her always close to his heart in secret.

The war passed more slowly than the years. There were prayer services and vigils and boys Jack had known coming home in coffins. There were funerals and memorial services. Michael Durkin, who had been a year ahead of Jack at school, came home because he went crazy, and Jack helped Mr Durkin build a special room for him with no sharp edges and a heavy door that locked from the outside. The room had a window through which food could be passed when Michael was having one of his spells.

Jack worked at being a Christian. He took as his motto a line from the Prayer of St Francis, ‘Not to be understood, but to understand.’ Where he had been a quiet man before, he now became almost silent. While he worked at odd jobs for people in town, he listened to everyone and heard about everybody’s problems. As he began listening more carefully, he found he was able to hear less of the words people said and more of the intent that hid behind them. He discovered the true motivations of his neighbors: which loved money, which loved prestige, which loved attention, which loved anger. He discovered that all were at heart driven by fear and hopeless self-love. He began to see what crazy things people were willing to believe if only it made the fault lie with someone besides themselves. He stopped visiting Fr Farrell about this time, partly because both men had grown busier and partly because he was impressed (though not yet convinced) by the gossip about Fr Farrell's drunkenness and weakness. Sometimes in his last years he spoke of this as his betrayal of Fr Farrell.

And one day Willie McCover returned to a hero's welcome. It was the summer of 1918, and the Americans were now shoulder to shoulder with the Canadians, French, British, and Belgians. Everyone knew the war was coming to a close. And here – after four years of sacrifice, after so many sons lost – here came a boy from our own town, from our own school, decorated for conspicuous bravery in battle. He had crawled in the darkness across an open space of land and thrown a grenade into machine gun nest, freeing his platoon from the trap that had pinned them down. Soon the story had him opening a hole in the German line, and he became the true reason for success at the second battle of the Marne, during which time he had actually been in a London hospital. He became the opposite of a scapegoat: the focus of everyone's joy at the successful close of the war. He was the brave son of the entire town, which, since he was an abandoned child, was in a certain sense true. Did he have news of so-and-so? Had he seen this boy, that boy? Everyone invited him to dinner, to parties, for evenings of cards or music. As the Grand Alliance pushed the Germans back over the Hindenburg line, his opinion was sought by everyone. How long would it take? Would the Germans hold out? Had he seen Field Marshall Foch, or General Pershing? T.E. Lawrence, the Red Baron? Which was faster, the Fokker Triplane or the Sopwith Camel? How big were the new tanks? Were the stories about the prisoner camps true? How big were the big bertha guns? What about those French girls? What were these Bolsheviks, what did that all mean? All sorts of questions that he could not possibly have known the answers to were presented for his verdict, which was accepted with happy deference. Arguments were settled with, 'That's what Willie McCover said.' The boys in town followed him about, and George MacDonald the barber gave him a piece of paper saying he would have free shaves as long as he lived. Even Judge Johnston came around. That November while the French were having their way at Versailles, Anne and Willie McCover were married in the little church outside of which they had consummated their love four years earlier.

The wedding was a "splendid affair" and "universally attended," said the old newspaper clippings. Fr Farrell presided over the ceremony. The newspaper account commented favorably on the priest's sermon on temperance in marriage, and added laconically, "he spoke with both hands firmly grasping the sides of the pulpit," surely a gibe at the priest's putative *delirium tremens*. Willie was dashing in a dress military uniform made specially for him by the tailor, and wore three medals on his breast. Anne's younger sister, who had moved to Toronto to take a job for the government, came with her new husband. Anne wore a cream-colored dress. A photograph shows that the couple walked up the aisle together, as was the custom before

Hollywood movies. The only thing we ever heard about the wedding from our relatives was from a distant great aunt, who told us, "It's a good thing she wasn't wearing white," and her husband, who shushed her and said that people were entitled to their mistakes.

The wedding reception was something we heard more about. Our great grandfather saw Judge Johnston and walked over to congratulate him.

"Willie McCover," said the Judge.

"The town's greatest soldier," said Jack.

"Willie McCover," said the Judge. He took out his pipe and lit it. "I couldn't do anything with her, Jack," he said. "She's not an easy girl to marry. It may take a Willie McCover," he said, and laughed. "She's not an easy girl to marry."

Jack had never thought of Anne in those terms. How could Anne not be an easy girl to marry? He had always thought of marrying her. He had a sudden vision of Anne sitting in a window waiting, then marrying Willie McCover because she thought no one else would have her. He felt dizzy and wandered away from the Judge. He wondered if he was drunk. But those were still the days of prohibition in Ontario, and there was no alcohol in the punch.

Jack found himself back inside the hall. A band from Peterborough was playing. He sat by himself to smoke and think. Couples waltzed past. Anne and Willie were making their way from table to table talking to the guests. They came to the table next to Jack, where Mrs Oliphant and some other ladies were sitting.

"We would like to thank you all for coming," said Anne. "Everyone has been so kind to us. I'm sure we don't deserve it all," and she took Willie's hand in hers. It seemed to Jack that he had never seen Anne so happy.

"There's an old saying, 'I'll dance at your wedding,' " said Mrs Oliphant, who had had not in fact danced. "I think it's always better late than never, you know, but of course I'm too old to do that sort of thing," she said. She meant, she said later, that although she was too old to dance it was better to attend a wedding late in life than not at all.

Willie said, "We're very grateful to you all for coming, Mrs Oliphant and all you ladies, to enjoy your company and your lovely dresses, and how wonderful I feel as a veteran of the service to come home to such a fine little town." The band had stopped playing, and since Willie had not said more than a few words all evening, his sudden speech captured everyone's attention. "I have seen the capitals of Europe, ladies and gentlemen," he said, growing expansive, "I have seen the great cities of America and the people they house. I have seen the trenches and shell holes, I have crossed the Hindenburg line with a rifle in my hand. You all, each and every one of you, honor us with your presence, even if it is just a free meal and a chance to gossip, and even if you are traitors and toothless hags who should just mind your own God-be-damned business, you bleeding old sluts," and he slammed his fist on the table.

"Willie, I'm sure Mrs Oliphant didn't mean,..." said Anne.

"And I've had it up to here with you crowd of backwater nobodies with sour milk in your veins and blood in your piss," he began to shout. "Blood in your piss!"

And so, surely to the delight of most of the town, the stories started before the wedding reception was over. Willie was drunk at the reception. He slapped Anne the night they were married. The most terrific shoutings and howlings came from their little house on the High Road at the edge of town. Willie drank. Willie's job kept him on the road for weeks at a time, but he stayed away even longer than he needed to, selling illegal alcohol and whoring. People talked to relatives, friends, and even strangers from the neighboring towns and heard tell of Willie McCover in hotels and speakeasies. Twice in their first year together Anne ran home crying to her parents, once with a black eye. On the second of these occasions she quarreled with her mother. Then she went back to Willie McCover for good.

The people in town were divided on the subject of Anne and Willie. Willie, after all, was a war hero like his father before him, and in 1919 people did not want to criticize anyone who had served overseas. "The boys went through a lot for us over there," they would say, as if Willie's behavior were justified by his war record. Not a few people were quick to point out that Anne was the kind who had it coming: "Her father always gave in to her," said Mrs Oliphant, "She's only getting now what she should have gotten as a little girl. If they had given it to her then, it wouldn't hurt so much now." Many people also remembered how they had been embarrassed by Anne's defiant introductions on the street several years before, how they disliked her snobbery ("She always thought she was better than the rest," was something Jack heard more and more), or how her father had ruled against them in court. They had to agree that Mrs Oliphant had a point. "Perhaps that Willie McCover will knock some sense into her," they would say.

But things deteriorated further after the first year. When Willie was home, he was often seen sitting on his front porch drinking, and he would wave at people walking past and invite them in for whiskey in a loud voice, then begin cursing and swearing, so that people stopped taking the High Road unless they were driving and instead walked the extra mile around on the forest road. By then people began to forget what Willie had done in the war, and they remembered instead his hard-drinking father and how Willie had been a wild boy in his youth.

Anne's mother died suddenly of a stroke in 1922. The daughter had not seen her mother for a year except at church, where they avoided each other's eyes and sat in pews on opposite sides of the centre aisle. No one needed to be told that their argument had been about Willie McCover. There was a reconciliation between father and daughter, and they attended the funeral together. Since Judge Johnston was the most prominent Catholic in town, and because his work brought him into contact with almost everyone at one time or another, nearly everyone attended the funeral. The only notable absence was the son-in-law, Willie McCover. Anne told everyone she met that Willie had wanted to come, but could not because he was out of town on business. He sent his regrets, she said. Her eyes were wide and red with tears.

After the funeral, most of the congregation gathered outside the church under the great oak tree in the cemetery. The casket had been lowered into the hole and Fr Farrell was saying the final prayer for the dead. It was a cold autumn day, and people were shivering in their newly fashionable trenchcoats. Colorful leaves swirled about, and the grave was filled with maple propellers and brown oak leaves.

People commented afterward on how strange it was that nobody stopped him when he first arrived. A car pulled up on the street while they were singing the *Salve Regina*. Willie McCover appeared, walking up the little hill to the cemetery, bottle in hand, bawling, "Pie in the sky, you get pie in the sky when you die!" The singers stopped. Willie had nothing against Mrs McCover, people said afterwards, who never did anything to him, and there was no need for him to hold a grudge against her just because of what she had said to Anne. But there he came, and no one stopped him or said anything. It was the shock of it, everyone agreed: no one was ready for such horrible disrespect for the dead. By the time Willie got to the casket Fr Farrell's mouth was hanging open. For a minute even Judge Johnston could only stare. "Let's have a drink!" yelled Willie. It seemed that he was going to pour his whiskey into the mouth of the grave, but he saw Judge Johnston and stopped.

"Get away from here," whispered the Judge, trying to find his voice. Everyone heard it, it was so quiet in the cemetery. His hand was full of earth that he had been about to drop over the coffin.

"Willie," said Anne, and tried to slip past the Judge – she was standing next to the grave, with her father between her and her husband.

"Away, get away!" shouted the Judge, and he grabbed Anne and shoved her into Willie, the dirt in his hand flying and smearing the sleeve of her coat. Then the spell was broken, and the men from the town were there, bustling Willie McCover away, helping Anne behind him, one even thinking to take Anne's lilies from her and come back to drop them on the grave, as was the custom.

Although no one said it, it was the most successful funeral the town had ever had.

Besides the funeral, Jack did not see Anne for more than a year. He was a busy man – Mr Quill had retired and Jack was now managing the bank – and besides, no one saw the McCovers. He took a different woman to the Saturday night dances at the parish hall, but nothing came of it, and it seemed that he was going to remain a bachelor all his life. Some of the people in town were disappointed in him, mostly women of his mother's generation: "Jack LeRoy is a good steady man. Why doesn't he do something with his life?" by which they meant marry or become a priest. "Not to speak ill of those who aren't, but the younger generation are the most selfish bunch I've ever seen," said Mrs Oliphant, who now worked for Jack at the bank. "I don't know what that Jack LeRoy is doing with his life," she would say, often in Jack's hearing.

Jack did not know what he was doing with his life either. After Anne's marriage, he had thrown himself into his work at the bank, gradually giving Mr Quill enough confidence to turn all the day to day business over to him. The work filled his days and kept him busy, and at his best times – during the long days of work – he felt like he was waiting, although he could not have said for what. At his worst times – generally Sunday afternoons after the church luncheon was over and there was no work to be done – he felt as though his life were sliding away from him, that the decisive moment of his life had come and gone without him noticing and was receding further into the past every day. He did not forget Anne, nor exorcise his feelings for her. Rather that part of him went to sleep, like a virus gone dormant, an enemy within that may never be heard from again, or may rise up and attack.

My great grandfather always began the next part of the story sitting in Toronto with Anne beside him on a Sunday afternoon. They had already been waiting for an hour, and there was no sign from the slow-moving policemen that they would be attended to any time soon. Anne had not told Jack exactly why they were there, but it was obvious that Willie was in some trouble.

That day Jack had found Anne waiting for him when he returned home after mass. Her face was made-up, and the make-up had smeared around her eyes – facts to which Jack attached no importance when he first saw her. He started to invite her in for tea, but she interrupted him and said, "I need to get to Toronto, will you drive me?" In the car, he learned that little Annie was with her grandfather, and that something had happened to Willie. They drove for two hours, stopped at a restaurant while Anne phoned for directions, and after several wrong turns they found the police station on Dundas Street, where they waited.

Again Jack tried to talk to Anne, but she made no reply. He could see that she was holding herself tightly: coiled like a spring, he thought. A screaming Chinaman with only one arm was dragged through the waiting area by two large policemen. Jack wondered what Willie could have done to be thrown into jail – women? Did they put you in jail for having too many women? Jack did not know. Perhaps Willie had gotten into a gambling fight, or gotten drunk. But were those serious enough to keep you in jail more than a day or two? Perhaps he had stolen something. Jack, normally sure of himself, felt suddenly embarrassed to be a man who knew so little of the world.

He looked at Anne, thinking, She is a strong woman. She wore a white hat and gloves that reminded him of her youthful promenades with Willie up and down King Street years before. Jack studied her while trying to appear as if he were not. Fortunately her grief was such that she did not notice. Her face was no longer the face of a young woman. There were the beginning of crow's feet around the eyes, and dark circles beneath them, and two lines slashing down from the nose around the mouth to the chin. For an instant, Jack saw the future of Anne's face, the collapsing cheeks of old age, the sagging eyes and mouth, the drooping jowls.

"Mrs McCover?" asked a policeman with a clipboard.

Anne stood up and nodded.

"This way," he said, and led them into a labyrinth of hallways, staircases and tunnels, turning so many times that Jack had no idea in which direction they were heading nor where the way out could be. The underground tunnel they walked through was made of concrete. There were boiler pipes running along the ceiling, and the air was hot and stifling. It seemed to Jack that they stayed underground for many city blocks. He would have liked to talk with the policeman, to ask him questions about the city and businesses there, but he did not speak out of respect for Anne, who was silent.

At last they came to a large room with metal tables on the floor and lights hanging down from the ceiling. A thick chemical smell hung in the air. On the tables under sheets were the corpses of men and women. There were men in white coats walking around the room with clipboards.

"McCover, McCover," said the policeman, and hailed one of the men in the white coats. "McCover?" he asked.

The man in the coat led them to a wall filled with huge file drawers. "McCover, McCover," he said to himself, as if the name were a song passing from man to man. Finally he said, "McCover." He opened one of the file drawers.

What Jack would always remember was Willie McCover's eyes. They were cracked open, glazed and pale blue. He Jack's throat constricted and his mouth became dry. The chemical smell made his head reel. He stared at Willie's eyes, at his sunken cheeks, his sagging chin. His mouth was a downturned slash, his lips grey. Although Jack knew that it was Willie McCover, he felt he would not have recognized him, death had so deformed his face. A short time before those eyes had seen the city, those feet had carried his body, the mouth had spoken and eaten and even kissed. Jack understood for the first time that sin was its own punishment. He could almost hear Willie whispering, "Too late, too late."

Jack mumbled a Hail Mary for Willie's soul to himself. He heard Anne's voice speaking, and the policeman asking questions, and the man in the white coat closed Willie's drawer.

There were papers to sign at the police station, and questions and statements. Jack could not concentrate while the policeman described the circumstances of death, and heard only the phrase that would be spoken of Willie McCover for decades afterward in his hometown, brought there by the salesman who took on Willie's territory: "died in a brothel."

Jack had too much to think about on the way home. They passed silently through the southern Ontario night, warm and inviolate in their car. The trees on either side sheltered and hid them as they passed, and the darkness wrapped around them like a coat. To Jack it seemed as though they might never have existed, so insulated were they from the world. He longed to beep the horn, to crash the car into a tree, to take a gun and shoot in the air, just to let the world know that he was in it, to be noticed once before joining Willie in his drawer. He recognized these thoughts as foolish. We all alike go into those drawers, he thought. What good does making noise do? He thought of the Last Judgment scenes from the illustrated bible he had read at school when he was a boy. At the end of the world, all the bodies of the dead would rise from their drawers and graves to meet near the ocean in a huge throng. He and Willie McCover would stand on the shore and meet Christ together.

Jack began to daydream as they drove. The eyes of Willie's corpse, which were slightly open, were blue. He had heard that all newborn babies had blue eyes, and he wondered idly whether all the dead had blue eyes as well. He was amazed at Anne, who had not cried nor even cried out when she saw Willie. He glanced over cautiously, not wanting to intrude on her grief. Her face was dry, and Jack once again marveled at her strength.

"How much life insurance did my husband have?" she asked him. Her voice was firm and sensible. It shocked him.

"I don't know. I'd have to talk to the insurance company," he said.

"What about his will? Is that with you?" she asked, meaning, was it with the bank? She asked about the mortgage, how to sell Willie's car, about the bank accounts, the fire insurance, and other money matters.

Without the files in front of him, Jack knew nothing about Willie's affairs, except that he was often late with his payments. He kept saying, "I'll have to see what arrangements Willie made," so that Anne became annoyed. "And just what is it that you do at that bank all week?" she asked. Jack was ready to tell her that she had just lost a husband, did nothing matter to her but money, when she said simply, "I'm just thinking of little Annie," and Jack stopped himself. Widows must be practical in these matters, he thought.

Jack did not like practicality in Anne, and he did not like it in himself. He found new thoughts in his mind, rustling and gnawing like rats in garbage. Anne McCover was now a single woman. They were still young. She deserved better than she had received. What had she had with Willie? Shouting, screaming, beating – not a moment's peace nor happiness. The first night of their marriage Willie had humiliated her before the entire town. Unlike Willie, Jack worked steadily, paid his bills, incurred no debts. He was kind and gentle. He did not swear, he had not been drunk in years. His wife would not have to travel to Toronto to find him dead from a brothel. Anne had fallen asleep on the seat beside him, and her orange hair was dark and fell mysteriously about her face in the glow of the car's instrument panel.

Jack shook himself. I learned of Willie McCover's death an hour ago, and I am already feeding on his corpse, he thought. He tried to say a Hail Mary for the dead man's soul, but his thoughts were running in all directions and he could not control them. He thought of little Annie, of Anne in her formal dress, of the blue crack of dead Willie's eyes, of Willie's speech at his wedding and Willie's song at the funeral of Anne's mother. He thought of Anne's businesslike questions. He looked over at her again, sleeping beside him in the car. Her mouth sagged with sleep, and she seemed vulnerable and lonely. How lovely she has always been, Jack thought. Then he shook himself again and cursed himself, and leaned forward over the steering wheel so that he would see only the road.

As they had for Anne's wedding, everyone in town came to Willie McCover's funeral. Judge Johnston and Anne sat together in the first row. Nancy came from Ottawa and sat with them, but this time her husband did not come. Nancy already had four children, her hips and waist had spread. She had blue- and green-tinged circles beneath her eyes.

Although she was younger than Anne by five years, she looked ten years older. Anne was dry-eyed at the funeral and held her head steady and high. She reminded Jack of a film he had seen in which the actress plays a priestess watching Rome burn: proud, sad, and defiant, as if all of this were no more nor less than she had expected. Little Annie sat with her family with red hair and a black dress that mirrored her mother's.

Willie McCover was given an obituary in newspapers as far as Toronto, where they only mentioned his war record and not the circumstances of his death. The name of our town was featured prominently. At the funeral people remembered his heroism, and the heroism of his father against the Indians in Texas. But even before they had rolled the casket out of the church, the stories were beginning: it had taken them a long time to find Willie because there were so many addresses to check, they found him in the bed of some strumpet, and the ageless joke about *rigor mortis* and in what organs Willie would be stiff until the end of time.

His sordid death was a triumph of sorts for the town. Jack was beset by questions for the details of the trip to identify Willie's body: what did Anne do when she saw the hotel, what did those Toronto girls look like, what actually goes on in places like the one Willie died in? When Jack began to describe the trip to the police station and the morgue, the smell of formaldehyde and the faces of the corpses, he was listened to with a respectful skepticism and then questioned further about the brothel. Was it true that they wore the kind of stockings and garters that you saw in the movies? Jack heard dirty jokes in his office at the bank, heard the stories at the grocery when he did his shopping, and the judgments at coffee after church on Sundays. "Just like his father, he came to a bad end. It wasn't as if this was unexpected," said Mrs Oliphant, and for the most part everyone had to agree.

When the stories about Willie began to grow tired, there was always Anne to talk about: "A headstrong and spoiled girl who got more than she bargained for," or even, "who got what she deserved."

It took ten years, but Anne and Jack were married. In time, little Annie had the brother who would become our grandfather and tell us their stories, and what he did not tell us we would fill in for ourselves, with facts from other sources and stories to bridge the gaps. My grandfather's recollection of his father and mother always stopped before he was born, and he rarely spoke about what his life as a child was like with them. When we were young, my sister and I thought that he ended the story there because that was the end of the story: Jack had waited fourteen years for his true love Anne and finally they had been married, and they lived happily ever after.

But we learned how she died, and we would later learn that little Annie ran away from home when she was seventeen and years later would become Wandering Annie, a notorious bag lady in Hull. We heard that from our uncle who was the grandson of Anne's younger sister, Nancy. Before Anne married Jack but after Willie McCover's death, she used gasoline to set fire to the house on the High Road, a crime for which she was not prosecuted. Later, in the early years of her second marriage, Anne tried on different occasions to burn down the barn on her father's property, the house she was born in, and later, the house where she lived with Jack and my grandfather. She was released into

Jack's custody each time. We discovered this only accidentally, by reading old newspapers and documents, and not from the carefully edited stories of our elders. She died on her first husband's grave when I was three years old. My only memory of her is of the piercing stare of wrinkled green eyes that made me cry and run to my mother – and even this may not be memory at all but only something I have been told so often that I seem to remember it.

If Anne went crazy, what kind of a man was Jack? How was he able to overlook all problems, and who, according to my grandfather's report, never said a harsh word to his wife, who, when she ran off to take food and read poetry to her long dead first husband, simply went to the cemetery to fetch her? Besides her pyromania and obsessions, my great grandmother would sometimes have uncontrollable fits of cursing, and may have suffered from what is now known as Tourette's Syndrome. She sometimes went weeks without speaking, and clearly had spells of clinical depression.

My grandfather, the first child of Jack and Anne's union, once said that Jack never really had any idea what kind of person his wife was. On another occasion he told us that neither of his parents had really looked at the other since before the First World War – Jack lived with a beautiful picture of Anne, and Anne barely noticed Jack despite their marriage.

The romantic rebels against the limitations of the world, she refuses to accept the mediocrity of her surroundings, she refuses to accept death, and, like Heathcliff, ends up haunting cemeteries looking for a ghost that is nothing more than a projection of her own egotism. There is no doubt that Jack did not see Anne the way she was, but saw rather the way she had been. One view sees this as the very romanticism that his wife exemplified and that Jack despised. Like his wife, Jack haunts the grave of his dead love, the high-spirited girl who died in the arms of Willie McCover beneath the great oak tree one night in the cemetery and rose a profoundly troubled woman. But another interpretation states the opposite, arguing that Jack in his humility saw Anne in the way Christ is said to see, not only the woman as she became in her pathology, sin, and pride, but the woman she ought to have been, captured forever in the vision of the beautiful young girl who stole his heart one afternoon in 1914. The mystics say nothing good is ever lost, because all good things are a part of God – was it this faith, and not blind egotism, that sustained Jack through thirty years of marriage to an insane woman who never loved him?

The last time I saw my great grandfather alive he lay in a hospital bed in the nursing home in Brighton. His face was grey and his hair was gone and although he had been a strong and well-built man throughout his life, he weighed less than 120 pounds in his last illness. I brought him cigarettes, which he craved but were forbidden. We talked about the city's eternally inept hockey team, the upcoming municipal elections, the Americans and their blundering foreign policy adventures.

"The romance of it, the romance of it," said my great grandfather. "Vietnam was all romance. The newspapers, the radio, the television... It all turns into romance, even our simplest things turn into lies. Oh the poor Americans, all good intentions that amount to horrors..." He faded out for several seconds as if he forgot what he was saying. Many of his pronouncements in that last year made more sense if you substituted the name of a person for the institution or country he was supposedly speaking of, and that this held true for empires and hockey teams both: he would be suddenly overcome by a sadness too personal for the topic that occasioned it.

His focus returned and he said, still putatively speaking of the Americans, "Vietnam. The old men betrayed them. Their own old men betrayed them."

I gathered later that he meant the generals and the politicians betrayed the soldiers they sent into battle, but at the time I had to ask whom he meant by 'the old men'. He was talkative but difficult to follow.

"Old men are the great betrayers. They have so little time, so little time. They want so much to think that their lives will continue that they refuse to face the simplest facts. The simplest facts. And when you lose one, you lose them all, you are unable to see the simplest truths of the world, of the way the world works. The first betrayal contains all betrayals..."

I told him not all old men betray – more out of condescension and, truth be told, fear of involving myself in his strong emotion.

"Oh, we all do in the end. We all do. There is nothing left in my life that, in my dark times here, I would not pawn for a few more years, a few more breaths. And yet, what would I have done differently? What else could I have done? I look back on the years and at what I knew and when I knew it, and how else could I have been, I was a child, a child, we are children all our lives, and the end comes and we want only to hide, the night fears of childhood come back and we pay for all our pride..."

He faded out of his speech and lay still for a time so that I thought he was sleeping, but when I looked his eyes were open and staring out the window. I was glad he had stopped talking, since I had my own strong vision of him, of what kind of man he had been and what kind of man he was, and I did not want him to destroy it at the last. We sat quietly together for several minutes. I watched the orange sun floating in his window like the angel of death.

It occurred to me that this might be the last time I saw him, because in a few days I was to return to school for the new semester. I wanted him to sit up, for the life to come back into his eyes and for him to tell me once more about his wife, the crazy and strong Anne Johnston: "Did I ever tell you," he would ask, "about the day I almost asked your great grandmother to the tea dance?" But the sun continued her downward course and the room grew dark. Soon I sat staring at the night outside his window. There was a streetlight in the park across the way and the leaves on the trees were silver with it. A nurse came to tell me that visiting hours were over, but I did not move and she went away. I sat by my great grandfather's bed for a time and listened to him snore. Then I stood up, kissed the transparent skin of his forehead and left him there.

They are buried together now in the ground beneath the stump of the old oak tree, not far from the place where Willie McCover lies.

Re-Statement of Romance

The night knows nothing of the chants of night.
It is what it is as I am what I am:
And in perceiving this I best perceive myself

And you. Only we two may interchange
Each in the other what each has to give.
Only we two are one, not you and night,

Nor night and I, but you and I, alone,
So much alone, so deeply by ourselves,
So far beyond the casual solitudes,

That night is only the background of our selves,
Supremely true each to its separate self,
In the pale light that each upon the other throws.

-Wallace Stevens
(1879-1955)

About the Author

J. Mulrooney was baptized at St Lawrence Church in Scarborough, Ontario, by Father Breen, and made his first communion some years later at Annunciation Parish in Don Mills. Sometime after that, he studied at St Michael's Choir School, then at St Michael's College at the University of Toronto, the Centre for Medieval Studies, and the Iowa Writers' Workshop. Besides this collection, he is the author of two novels, *23 Winters in Rochester, NY* and *An Equation of Almost Infinite Complexity*.

If he has not died yet, Mr. Mulrooney is likely still living in Irondequoit, NY.

37226593R00131

Made in the USA
Lexington, KY
22 November 2014